FIREFLIES

MELISSA KOBERLEIN

Parker West Books

Parker West Books
www.parkerwestbooks.com

ISBN: 978-0-9891425-4-0
Parker West Books

Printed in the United States of America

August 2016

PROLOGUE

Centuries ago, a large meteorite fell from the sky. Searching for a new home, it floated through space and time, finally coming to rest in the middle of a planet surrounded by land, water, and life. Hidden by trees and brush amidst the Appalachian Mountains in the northeastern part of the United States, an extraordinary vessel waited to be discovered. No human could imagine or prepare for what lie within its depths. Until one day, a curious, lone hiker pushed aside one small branch, and a new species was born on Earth...

1

CONTACT

Will

Present Day

I've been tracking humans my entire life. While each time is different, it's always the same rush.

Pennsylvania is unseasonably warm this April. I reach for an evergreen branch, the sharp needles pricking at my palm. It has been too long since I've been here. I close my eyes, breathing deeply the calming earthy scents of my home woods: pine, cedar, grass, algae on some rocks of a nearby stream, fresh water trickling down, and a distance away, violet wild flowers. Focused and determined, I open my eyes, smiling eagerly.

I'll find my quarry.

I reach down and press my palm to the ground. Images pass through my mind like frames in a movie. Two girls passed through here, one brunette, one blonde, both searching for something...another girl, a friend. They're local high school students about the same age as me, on a trail cleanup detail. The girl they're searching for has fallen into a ravine. She's afraid, but not seriously hurt.

Standing, I begin my hike, following the two girls in search of their friend. Five hundred feet up the trail, I catch up to them. Quickly, I hide behind a tree, my t-shirt scraping the bark.

It's her. The one I've been tracking. I've got to mark her to let the others know she's mine. Slowly, as if not by my own will, I step back onto the path to get a better look. She's navigating the trail as if she were born to hike, reassuring and leading the girl behind her. I feel an instant pull as my heart pounds from being this close to her. My instinct is to approach her now, but that would be foolish. I need to wait for the perfect time. Besides, she's focused on her lost friend. In fact, she's almost to the top of the ravine.

I consider yelling up to them, when she stops and turns toward me. Instinctively, I duck back behind the tree just in time, each breath coming fast and furious. I lean my head against the tree, closing my eyes, concentrating. She knows I'm here.

The brunette says, "What's up, Marley?"

"I thought I saw something," the blonde replies.

"I'm sure it's probably some other kids looking for Becca," the dark-haired girl says.

The blonde's name is Marley, and her senses are impeccable for a human.

They continue moving up the trail as I silently follow. I can't lose sight of her, not even for a second.

I want this one, and no one is going to take her from me.

Marley

"Where do you think she could have gone?" Liz asks for what seems like the hundredth time.

I stop and turn to face her. Liz Larson has been my best friend ever since the first day of kindergarten, when she offered to share her dad with me since I didn't have one. She's not easily rattled, but now, out here, she looks terrified.

"Don't worry. We'll find Becca. Besides, she's only been lost for about half an hour."

"But, where is she?" Liz urges, panic still evident in her bright blue eyes.

"Liz, I know every square inch of this place."

We live in the town of Pine Grove, amongst farmland and the Appalachian Mountains in central Pennsylvania. I've been hiking the trails since I was five; they're practically my second home. However, glancing up at the ominous clouds, I realize we have a more pressing problem. The heat on the ground is causing instability in the sky.

"Do you see those dark clouds? We need to find Becca before they open up. Now let's get going."

Liz nods, her dark ponytail bobbing in agreement. Liz isn't the kind of girl who would enjoy being caught in the rain.

A few more feet and I hear her. I stop dead in my tracks, and Liz, who doesn't realize it, stumbles into me. "Ouch, what—"

I grab her and cover her mouth with my hand, my eyes telling her to be quiet.

She stiffens, but understands.

I mouth, "Listen," and remove my hand.

The distinct sound of crying floats on the air. It's not far.

Hope returns to Liz's eyes. "Becca, Which way?"

I close my eyes, trying to focus on the crying, but a strange feeling that someone is watching us intercedes.

I open my eyes and glance behind Liz on the trail. For the second time, I see someone or something for a split second. *Who's out there, and why are they following us?*

Liz follows my line of sight. "What are you looking at?"

"I'm not sure. I thought I saw someone." As soon as I say the words, I wonder if I'm imagining things.

"Becca?"

"No...something else."

Liz turns back to face me. "Stop trying to scare me, Marley. I don't see anyone."

"Have you ever had the feeling that someone was watching you? I can't shake it..."

Liz swats my arm. "Snap out of it! You're really freaking me out! Where's Becca?"

I shake my head and refocus. It's starting to drizzle. "Yeah, sorry...it's this way." I point off the trail to our right. "The crying is coming from down there in the ravine. If you want to stay up here on the trail, I'll go."

"Okay, I'm not moving from this spot. Just please hurry up and come back with Becca."

"I'll be right back." I grab the branch of a low birch tree and swing myself down into the dense underbrush. *No snakes. Please, no snakes.* I continue making my way down into the ravine, carefully grabbing branches to steady myself, as the crying grows louder. It's definitely her.

"Becca, I'm coming!" I shout.

As soon as my feet hit level ground, I practically fall over my good friend, Becca Wright.

"Marley! Oh my God, thank you for finding me!" Becca cries.

"How did you end up down here? Why didn't you stay with the class?" I demand, my tone serious.

"I took a break to read...wasn't watching where I was going. I fell, and then I fell some more. I tried to get up, but my ankle really hurts." Her eyes are pink and puffy from crying, and there are leaves stuck in her hair. I may have been a little harsh.

Plucking a rather large leaf from the top of her head, I bend down next to her. We need to get back to the trail as soon as possible. I swallow hard and pull down her sock to look at the damage as the drizzle turns into light rain. Her ankle is swollen, but she can move it. I exhale the breath I was holding. Thank God. The queasiness from seeing her already darkening ankle passes. No blood. No bones. It's only a sprain, but there's no way she's going to be able to walk on it.

"Okay, the hill is way too steep for me to try and hold you up. We could both fall and make things worse. Can you crawl?"

"I don't think so. I can't put any pressure on my ankle." Tears well up in her eyes again.

I nod. Plan B. I grab a rope from my backpack. "So here's what we're going to do. I'm going to tie this around your waist and pull you as you push with your good leg. We'll have to inch our way back up to the trail. You ready?"

Becca glances up as rain washes the salty tear stains off

her cheeks. "I don't care what we have to do. Just please get me out of here."

I flash an encouraging smile. "I got you, Bec. Don't worry." I tie the rope around her waist and pull her toward the incline, which looks much more vertical from down here. With Becca sitting, facing away from me, we begin our trek back up the hill. The sky rumbles, and I know we only have a few minutes left until the torrential downpour.

Pull...slide...pull...slide...pull...slide.

On and on we go, until I see the tips of Liz's black boots. Phew! My breathing is ragged from exertion, and my arms and legs are on fire. I couldn't make it much further. Even though I'm a strong hiker and climber, I've never had to drag someone out of a ravine and in the rain to boot!

"Liz! Grab this and pull!" I toss the end of the rope to her.

"Got it!" she yells back, beginning to tug Becca.

I slip down past Becca, pushing her upward. The rain picks up, creating a muddy slide down into the ravine. A few more pushes and she should be out.

"I've got her!" Liz yells down as rain pelts my face and hair.

I sigh, relieved, taking a much needed deep breath. She's safe. "Okay, hang on, I'm coming!"

I grasp a branch from a bush and pull myself to my feet. A surprising surge of vertigo hits, and I sway, my head swimming. I pull on the branch for support, trying to regain my footing, but it snaps. I'm in the air, falling backward.

Down I go, sliding through mud and branches, until I hit the bottom of the ravine with a thud.

Ouch! I roll onto my side, groaning.

I sit up and quickly check my body for injuries. I'm going to be a little bruised up, but nothing is broken.

"Marley! Are you okay?" Liz yells from somewhere above me.

"I'm okay, you guys. Liz, take Becca back down the trail. I can't climb back out until the rain stops. Don't worry, I'll be fine!"

Liz replies, "Okay, I'll be right back!"

"Okay..." I whisper to myself, wondering what I should do while I wait.

I look down. I'm coated in mud. For once the extra set of clothes in my bag will come in handy. When it stops raining, I'll change and figure out which way is the easiest to get back up to the trail. At least it's not cold. The rain continues, and I'm glad for it. It's cleaning the mud out of my hair and off my face and hands.

I reach into my bag for my canteen. A few swigs later I feel better.

Now, I wait.

A half an hour passes and the rain finally subsides. In the privacy of the ravine, I carefully pull my t-shirt off and shuffle out of my cargo pants. They're filthy with mud. I deposit them in a plastic bag pulled from my backpack. Luckily my bra and underwear are in good shape, albeit damp. I pull out a towel to dry my face and hands when I sense something... again. Someone or something is nearby. But this time is different; this time, I'm wearing nothing but my bra and underwear.

"Liz? Is that you?" I yell, nervously.

No answer.

Quickly, I cover my chest and reach for the clean clothes

in my backpack. I pull a t-shirt over my head and inch clean shorts up over my legs. As I lace up my boots on a nearby rock, I get the overwhelming feeling that something isn't right.

I stand, listening.

There's no noise. No birds, no bugs, nothing. The air has fallen eerily still.

The next thing I know, the ground trembles underneath my feet. I stumble and drop to my knees. My body heats, and the sun, still behind the clouds, can't be to blame. My forehead is on fire, sweat dampening my hairline almost instantly.

I look down at the rock, and it moves. No, it dissolves... into nothing. Next, the ground moves and is gone too!

This is no earthquake... "Help!" I yell, knowing no one is within earshot.

I'm dizzy...so dizzy. I can't tell up from down and right from left.

I shake my head, trying to make the dizziness stop, but it won't. The encounter continues, the dizziness getting worse and worse...

A wave of nausea washes over me. I close my eyes to block out the haze, hoping I don't start puking.

Even more intense heat and the telltale tingling of adrenaline rushes through my veins. My body is reacting to something traumatic, but I have no idea what. I grasp out for something solid, but come up with nothing.

My heart pounds so hard, I think it might burst out of my chest.

My eyes flutter open, and I'm in shock. The ravine is completely gone...

I'm floating in nothingness. It's as if the world has melted away and left only me. I'm so scared I can't even scream.

I can't take any more...

As I begin to drift into unconsciousness, I feel pressure... intense on my left shoulder as someone or something presses down on me. I jump at the contact, but then relax as the heaviness turns to comfort and warmth. It's the only thing that is real.

After a time, I hear a deep voice in my head, *"Don't be afraid."*

My heart stops pounding and returns to its normal thump-thump as the space around me stops churning, and the ground of the ravine comes back into focus. I take a few deep breaths, filling my lungs, and grasp the smooth hardness of the large rock before me, reassuring myself that it's real.

I turn to see who or what touched me.

No one is there. I'm alone in the muddy ravine.

2

ONYX STONE

Will

I check my rearview mirror for the fifth time as I cruise down the mountain in my black 370Z, back toward civilization. What a rush! I wanted to celebrate my expertise right after the marking, but I had to get off the trails unnoticed. Quickly, I made it out of the ravine and waited long enough to ensure she also made it out. Then I worked my way back down to my car in record time. Damn, I'm good, if I do say so myself. There were a ton of Pine Grove High students blocking my exit to the parking area. Luckily, their class is large. They didn't pay particular attention to me since I look like any other seventeen-year-old boy. In fact, I think I blended in nicely. Go Hawks! What a change from the last school I attended, where everyone knew each other.

Marley. The moment I laid eyes on her, I knew she was the one I was hunting. I approached her stealthily and used my keen senses to my advantage. I tried to stay out of sight, but for some reason, she sensed my pursuit. I know for certain she felt the effects after I slipped down into the ravine and stood behind her, blocking out all other sounds except her to maintain my focus. As soon as I touched her, the familiar glow emanated from my hand and into her shoulder. Her breathing indicated she was experiencing some serious side effects; stronger than most potential humans I've marked in the past. I tried to calm her as best I could.

I sensed something special about her right away, almost familiar. For starters, she knows what she's doing on the trails —my kind of girl. Also, she looks great in her underwear. Obviously, she thought she was alone, and I knew I should have looked away, but I...well, I didn't. In fact, I couldn't take my eyes off her. There was something about the way she combed her curly blonde hair with her fingers. Those intense gray eyes, looking up when she sensed she wasn't alone and her muscular, tan legs...well, hopefully, if all goes according to plan, she'll prove to be strong. I wonder what she'll be like once she joins us...wait, I'm getting way ahead of myself.

I shake my head, needing to focus on driving. I inhale slowly, gripping the steering wheel a little tighter, thinking about what needs to be done. First on my list: meet her.

As soon as I pull into the driveway of my new house, I see a familiar car parked out in front. Oh, come on! Let the harassment begin. But, I guess that's what he's paid to do. Agent Jeffrey Rushmore emerges from his inconspicuous silver four-door sedan, wearing his usual black suit and aviator-style sunglasses. Do I detect a tan?

"Good afternoon, William," he says with authority.

William? Hmm, this is going to be official. "Agent Rushmore, good afternoon. Have you been vacationing? That's some tan. Who's the lucky girl?"

Agent Rushmore stares, unresponsive, as I walk over to him.

"What brings you to Pennsylvania?" I ask, already knowing the answer.

"Cut the crap, Will. What are you up to now? I needed you to stay put. There is an ongoing investigation, and you and your family just cut and run? This is not a game to me, young man. You better explain yourself."

Thanks to our special abilities to speak with one another, I know he has approached my dad and sister and turned up empty-handed. My mom is out of state, so he won't be getting any information from her. "Jeff, you know we like this area. I'm taking a break, stretching my legs. There's nothing going on here. I'll let you know if there is. Cool?" I try to smooth things over as best as I can. My dad is much better at this sort of thing.

Jeff Rushmore looks up and down the street and shakes his head. He takes off his sunglasses and approaches me until we are toe to toe. "I know you and your family are part of a top-secret extraterrestrial project, and you have special abilities, but don't think I'm stupid. I know perfectly well that you are always looking for potential humans to join you. So don't lie to me. The last time you did, I had to clean up a giant mess."

I glance down, unable to maintain eye contact. He's right, of course. My last tracking assignment was a disaster.

Jeff shifts his weight from one foot to the other. "Look, I like you and your family. But I have a job to do, and you are making it very difficult. So here's the bottom line: if I hear one peep about you breaking regulations or not registering a newbie, you and your whole family will be gone. I will have you deported. There will be no more stretching your legs in the United States of America. Do we understand each other?"

I know he means it, but he's only being hard on me because he feels out of the loop, which he is. "Got it, Jeff. I will check in with you. I will toe the line, blah, blah, I got it. Are we cool?" I stretch out my arms in a peaceful manner.

He seems to consider what I've said and then nods. "Yeah, okay. But I need to be sure we understand each other."

"Can we go inside now and have some food? My dad just finished grilling some steaks, and he added one for you." Hopefully, all the unpleasantness is behind us.

Jeff looks taken aback by my offer, but then his eyes soften. "Well, if it's not too much trouble. I love a good steak, and your father sure can cook."

"Of course, Jeff, let's go. I'll have my sister set a plate for you," I say as we walk up the sidewalk. The less he knows at this point, the better. I suspect another of us is getting help from someone on the inside at the FBI, and that is why our last mission failed miserably. We have to be extra careful now when we pass information to Agent Rushmore. He may tell the wrong person, and we will lose another one. That would be unacceptable.

Throughout dinner, all I can think about is Marley. Sure I've recruited plenty of potential humans, but never have I felt such a pull toward one. She's different from others I've met, yet somehow I feel like I've known her before. It's almost like deja vu. Either way, I've got a good feeling about this assignment, and something inside me can't wait to get started...

Marley

MAKING it back out of the ravine was a piece of cake compared to driving home. My hands are still shaking on the steering wheel as I pull into the driveway of a small colonial house in a modest neighborhood with tree-lined streets. I look up at my hundred-year-old house, wondering how much I should tell my mom, if anything.

The scent of lasagna wafts into the living room as I walk through the front door. Quietly, I move to the pot of sauce on the stove, next to my mom, allowing the aroma to wash away some of my anxiety about the incident. My imagination runs wild. What could it have been?

My mom smiles. "How was your day?"

She always asks this question, and I always reply 'fine,' but not today. I grab a seat on a stool at the counter opposite her. "Well, Becca got lost on our trip. She fell down into a ravine on Murphy Trail. Anyway, Liz and I found her, but..." I hesitate, not sure how much more I should explain. Honestly, I don't even know if I *could* explain. I decide on the truth, just not the whole truth. "...then I fell down into the ravine and got stuck waiting out the rain at the bottom."

My mom's eyes turn serious as she goes into robo-nurse mode, inspecting me for injuries. "Are you all right? Are you hurt? What about Becca?"

I bat at her prying hands. Having a nurse for a mom can be both a blessing and a curse. She always knows what's wrong, but she can get overprotective too. "I'm fine, and so is Becca. She's got a sprained ankle, but it could've been worse."

"You must be more careful out there. I know you love it, but you're giving me gray hair."

I can't help but roll my eyes. 'Out there' is the one place I really *do* know what I'm doing. I may not be the best at navigating the social paths at school, but out on the trails, I'm an expert. I'll never give it up. "I *am* careful, Mom. You don't have to worry."

She eyes me for a few more seconds. "I know you're very adventurous, but sometimes I wonder if you are a little too brave for your own good."

Me? Brave? Not today. She should have seen me at the bottom of the ravine when I didn't have any clothes on, and the world disappeared. I was anything but brave then.

My stepdad, Ray, interrupts our conversation, coming in the back door. He gives her a quick peck on the lips. "Smells delicious, Susan. How long?"

My mom smiles. "Ten minutes."

"What's new, Marley?" Ray squeezes my shoulder on his way to turn on the news in our usual ritual at dinner time.

"Hey, Ray," I reply, eyeing my mom, urging her to not say anything. "Nothing."

My mom shrugs her shoulders in compliance.

As we dig in, there's a story on about a boy from Austin, Texas. He's been missing for three weeks. He's my age and apparently he had a promising future. He went to bed one night and was gone the next morning. His parents are offering a reward for anyone who can give information about his whereabouts.

The boy's mother pleads with the camera. "Here's a picture of our son, Sam Wyatt. Please, if you've seen him, call the number at the bottom of your screen. Sam, if you're watching this, we miss you and want you to come home." She begins crying as the boy's father hugs her, and they turn away.

The reporter repeats the phone number to call. I sigh and swallow my last bite of lasagna. This is why I don't like watching the news. It's always bad.

After dinner, I head up to the solace of my room in the attic. My room represents me perfectly, probably because I renovated it myself, with some help from Ray. I kick off my shoes, digging my toes into the softness of the green area rug that reminds me of grass. My walls are painted white with pictures I took while hiking and some snapshots with friends. Oddly, I also have one of those old fox hunting paintings with the dogs and riders on horses. I can't quite explain why, but something about it appeals to me. I snagged it during the move to this house—it used to be in our old living room. The last item on my wall is a shelf that holds all of my old trophies from various sports I tried and eventually quit as a kid, including softball, swimming, and bowling. For me, the attic is my own private oasis, and it runs the entire length of the house.

I plop down on my queen-sized bed with tons of pillows, thinking I better get my homework done while I have the motivation. Rummaging through my bag for my biology book, I find a strange-looking stone at the bottom. I roll it back and forth in my hand. Black like onyx, with streaks of fluorescent green, and cool to the touch. How did it get in here?

Then it hits me. My backpack was in the ravine when I felt the strange dizziness and tremors.

As I study the stone, feeling the smoothness of it, the little fluorescent streaks glow, and it grows warm in my palm. It's relatively small, about the diameter of a nickel. I rack my brain, trying to figure out what this could be. Duh! Google. I grab my laptop, a precious birthday present from last year, and type in the words *onyx stone*. After sorting through a ton of irrelevant sites, I learn that onyx is a type of stone often used in jewelry and in building materials. It's predominately found in Mexico, Arizona, and Algeria. I add fluorescent streaks to the search box and come up with opals. Hmm, maybe the stone I have is more like a combination of the two or something.

After seeing an ad on the side of one of the sites about moonstones, brilliance strikes. I type in the word *meteorite*. The more I read, the more I believe that's what I have. There doesn't seem to be any stone or mineral found on Earth that looks anything like what's in my hand. I'll take it to school on Monday and show it to Mr. Bradshaw, during seventh period; he might have some idea about what it is.

I touch my left shoulder where I felt the mysterious pressure. My skin tingles. Standing in front of my mirror, I pull my shirt aside. What I see is nothing short of extraordinary. There's an outline of a circle on my skin, a mark where I felt something touch me. That's not all I see, though. Tiny speckles of fluorescence, like fireflies, radiate from the center of the circle.

"Mom!" I yell toward the stairs, not taking my eyes off my reflection.

A minute later, my mom's at the bottom of the stairs leading to my room. "What?"

"Come look at this!"

"What's wrong? You sound upset," she says breathlessly.

"Look." I turn toward her, my shoulder exposed.

She grasps my arm, examining my shoulder. "Where?"

She looks up and down my arm. "Does it hurt? Is it from the fall?"

"What are you talking about? It's right there!" I look back at my reflection in the mirror. Sure enough, the mark is still there.

"Marley, I don't see anything, but that doesn't mean there isn't a bruise there. It may be a day or so before you see it."

"You don't see anything on my shoulder? You're sure?"

My mom takes another close look at my shoulder and shakes her head. "No, Marley, I don't see anything. Are you sure you didn't hit your head?"

Uh-oh. I'd better back up, or I could land myself in the ER. "No, I didn't hit my head," I say calmly, pulling my shirt back up over my shoulder. "I guess I'm being a baby."

"Oh, Marley. This is what I'm talking about. You have to be more careful out there. Get some sleep, and I'll check it tomorrow if it's still really bothering you." She turns to head back downstairs.

"All right. Night, Mom."

After she's gone, I look back in the mirror at my shoulder. Why is my skin glowing? And why can't my mom see it? Am I hallucinating?

No, I can't be. The event happened. I know it. How else could that strange stone get in my backpack?

Tracing the fluorescent circle with my finger, I realize I'm not asking the most important question. Who or what touched me and why?

3

RECONNAISSANCE

Marley

Although the small clearing is a part of the woods I'm not familiar with, it feels like I've been here before. I look up at the sky, the position of the sun telling me it's mid-afternoon. The air feels warm, almost like summer, but there's no humidity. Everywhere I look, I see impenetrable evergreens and no path, no escape from the clearing I now stand in. I look down, and realize I'm wearing my nightgown and no shoes.

As soon as I move toward the trees, they part as if they have a mind of their own. It's frightening, but I need to move. I detect the unmistakable scent of moss and water coming from somewhere ahead. The grass is surprisingly soft under my bare feet as I make my way uphill to another clearing with a small pool surrounded by trees and brush. I bend down at the edge of the water, peering in. The water is black, but so still it mirrors my reflection. A rustling to my right startles me upright.

"Who's there?" I wish I had boots on.

The rustling stops, but my gaze never leaves the tree line. A squirrel wanders out from underneath a bush with an acorn. I breathe, not realizing I had been holding my breath. "You scared me, little squirrel."

The squirrel studies me for a few seconds and then bounds back under the brush. I look back down at the pool. My reflection is still there, but that's not all. Two glowing lights float on the surface. They remind me of something, but I can't think of what. Without warning, my shoulder hurts. I reach up, but a strong, masculine hand beats me to it. Gasping, I attempt to turn around, but I'm pulled back to the chest of the person behind me, a soothing feeling radiating into my shoulder. I can't think, feeling euphoric from the gentle massage, and the ache turns into something else.

I turn my head to look at the person behind me who feels so familiar. Everything is blurry, but it's a boy with strange piercing black eyes. He frightens me. I push away and fall into the pool...down into darkness. I struggle, fighting to come up for air, but can't seem to break the surface. I can't breathe...

I can't breathe!

I sit up in bed, trying to catch my breath. Instinctively, I touch my shoulder. The glow disappeared hours after the incident on Friday. It's even possible I imagined the entire thing. I swing my legs over the side of my bed and stand, stretching. I need to get a grip. It was only a dream.

Sunlight comes in through my fan-shaped windows at the other end of the attic. I jump a second time as my alarm clock beeps loudly. I turn it off at a lightning speed.

Falling back onto my bed, I give myself one last thought

about the dream. The hands felt familiar, almost as if they had touched me before. I groan, stretching my arms above my head. Back to reality.

I have school today.

Will

I pull into the parking lot of Pine Grove High early, hoping to catch a glimpse of Marley. I'm curious to see how she's been doing since our encounter in the ravine. The parking lot is filling up, and apparently, according to the man directing cars, students who drive have reserved parking spaces by grade. He gives me a temporary pass and directs me to one of the parking lots. Unfortunately, by the looks of the students getting out of the cars, my spot is on the other side of the school with the sophomores and teachers. Bad break— Marley's a junior.

As I get out of my car, I consider my next play. I've got to meet her, and it needs to be somewhat private on the off chance she got a look at me on the trails. I can't allow her to question me in front of others. The threat of exposure could cause my eyes to light up and give me away. Our secrecy from the general population is imperative, at least for now.

Let's see... I'm supposed to report to the office, and then go to my assigned homeroom. There won't be much privacy in a classroom filled with students. Wait...a smile spreads across my lips. Of course! Why go to her, when she could come to me?

Just as I'm about to work out the details of my plan, I notice two girls wearing cheerleading uniforms, walking toward the side entrance of the school, staring at me. One almost trips over her own feet. The other one giggles.

"Morning, girls," I say, broadening my smile further.

Neither replies. Instead, they both blush and hurry into the school. Once they're inside and out of normal human earshot, I hear one say that I'm *bangable*.

It's flattering, I guess. I run my hand through my hair one last time and straighten my jacket. I don't know why, but I want to make a good impression with Marley. I like her.

Then, as if she's standing right next to me, I hear Marley's voice coming from the other side of the school. My heart stops. I fight every urge inside me to go to her. It's not even a matter of simply being attracted to her; it's a primal need that only my kind experiences. I bend over, pressing my palms on my thighs, overcome, trying to catch my breath. Damn, she has an effect on me!

I have to concentrate. Focus. Slowly her voice shapes into words that I can recognize, my unique hearing better than most of my kind. She's talking with some other kids in front of the school. Something about a biology test. Her friend, Liz, from the trail, is there too. Liz heard that I moved in next door to their friend Becca and should be starting school soon. She's encouraging Marley toward me. Well, at least I know I have her as an ally. The group enters the school, and I realize I should be scanning the other students' conversations in the main hall. Closing my eyes and leaning against the brick exterior, I sort through the many voices carrying throughout the halls. The jumbled voices separate, and I'm able to hone in on one particular conversation I had hoped to avoid.

A group of students is discussing my fight with Joe Rein-hart. Of course, the news would travel fast. It's not a really small town, but people talk. It was simply a matter of being in the wrong place at the wrong time. I was in my new front yard when I heard this jerk call a girl, who I later realized was his girlfriend, a stupid whore! I interceded and pushed him. After he had taken a swing at me, missing, I reciprocated. I knew as soon as my fist connected with his left eye that it was a mistake. I'm supposed to be lying low, and instead I made a spectacle of myself. I can only hope that my mistake doesn't have any serious consequences with Marley's opinion of me. What will she think about me when she hears I hit one of her classmates? She might even be friends with the guy. No way. I refuse to believe that Marley would ever be close with anyone who would call someone a whore.

The hallways are emptying as I make my way inside the school and up to the office. I close my eyes to steady myself. I have to let it go. *What's done is done. Think positively. She's no different than any of the others. Win her. You've done this your whole life.* I open my eyes, regaining focus. I succumb to one last emotional thought. She *is* different.

I open the door to the office and smile shyly at the assistant typing away on her computer. A little 'lost boy' charm should rustle up an escort to my new homeroom in no time.

Let her come to me…

4

A NEW STUDENT

Marley

I slide into my seat and wait for the first bell to ring. Our homeroom and civics teacher, Mrs. O'Leary, is a very pretty woman originally from California. She likes to reminisce about her time living there. Word has it that she went through a messy divorce and needed a change in lifestyle. That's when she first came to Pine Grove two years ago. She's in charge of a lot of community projects. She likes me because I volunteer a lot, especially for trail stuff. I've done tours for kids and led cleanup details.

Liz turns around. "Do you think the new boy starts school today? I didn't see anyone out in the parking lot."

I didn't see anyone either, but then I wasn't really looking. "I guess you'll have to wait and see, Liz. Do you think you'll be able to handle the wait?" I ask, with mock sympathy.

"Yeah, you can occupy me," she retorts. "Oh, I forgot to tell you, I talked to Becca, and she said that he's got a sister too. She's in tenth grade." Then, in a more serious tone, "You know, you can tell a lot about people by their actions. I like that the new boy put Joe Reinhart in his place. We need some fresh ideas here; it's been getting terribly dull lately. Also, it doesn't hurt that you might get a boyfriend out of it too."

Leave it to Liz to be prophetic and state the obvious all at once. Not to mention, generous. A boyfriend?

"Listen, I don't want you to get your hopes up too much. You realize I'm more outdoorsy than most *guys* at our school, don't you? I don't think someone who is being called *bangable* is going to be my type. Besides, do you know how many single girls are in this school? More importantly, what if he already has a girlfriend or what if he's gay? Have you thought about any of these things?" I put my head in my hands, thinking about all of the events from Friday afternoon—the hand, the stone, the little lights. I tilt my head back up, combing my fingers through my too-wavy hair. Stupid humidity. "Besides, I have bigger problems. I forgot a ponytail holder."

Liz opens her mouth to respond, but she's interrupted by Mrs. O'Leary asking everyone to take his or her seat. The phone rings by the door, and she goes to answer it. As she listens to the person on the phone, she looks in my direction, waving me to the front of the room. Uh-oh, I haven't done anything wrong, have I? Who's she talking to on the phone? Quickly, I scramble out of my seat, only to trip over Liz's book bag, almost sending me flying across the floor. Luckily, I'm able to stop my fall by grabbing onto her desk. Embarrassed, I shoot her a sour look. Why the hell did she put her book bag in the middle of the aisle?

She cringes and silently mouths, "Sorry."

I steady myself and continue my trip up to Mrs. O'Leary. I

don't like being the center of attention or worse yet, in trouble.

"Mrs. O'Leary? Is there something wrong?" I ask quietly.

She looks annoyed but gives me a quick, dismissive smile. "No, no, Marley, there's nothing wrong. You have a permission slip to sign in the office for trail cleanup next week, and there is a new student who needs an escort back to our homeroom. Would you mind?"

"No, I mean, sure, okay..." I stammer, looking down at my sneakers. Ah, the new boy. Why did she pick me to go? I'm not exactly looking my best today. *Ugh. Get a hold of yourself, girl. What do you care?* He's just some stupid boy. On the other hand, he might actually be a cool person. Hmm... maybe if I take a detour...put some lip gloss on...try to fix my hair... Do I have time for that? The bell is going to ring soon. I have Calculus for my first period, and I hate being late for things...

"Marley?"

"Uh-huh?"

"The office? Permission slip? New student?" Mrs. O'Leary stares at me expectantly.

I'm still standing in front of her, daydreaming. God, I'm embarrassing. I shake my head, coming back to reality. "Oh, sorry, I'm going."

I hurry out of the room, but before I close the door I spot Liz giving me a thumbs up. Making sure only she can see me, I jokingly extend my middle finger in response.

I walk toward the office with purpose. I can't help but feel some butterflies in my stomach about meeting him. Hopefully he's nice, and I don't say anything stupid. I chuckle to myself. *Good luck with that.* Within minutes, I'm outside the glass-encased office. I approach the door, placing my hand on the knob. Suddenly, the hall swirls and the floor shakes. I shake my head, but the spinning won't stop. My mind travels to last Friday in the ravine. The spinning gets worse, and I know I need to sit down, or I'm going to pass out. There's no place to sit in the hall except the floor, so I turn the knob and push open the door.

A boy standing at the office counter turns to face me. As soon as his pitch-black eyes meet mine, everything fades to black.

Will

I grab Marley just before her head hits the floor, hoisting her up in my arms. What the hell? This isn't part of my plan! I've never had someone react so severely. Stupid! What was I thinking, surprising her like this?

"Oh my goodness, Marley!" one of the assistants in the office yells from behind the counter, snapping me back to my current predicament.

"I think she's okay. She fainted. If you could tell me which way to the nurse's office, I'll take her there to get checked out," I say, hoping the secretary will let it go at that.

Luckily, she does. After she gives me directions I don't actually need, I head out of the office carrying Marley, willing her to wake up. I have experience with the marking process and its effects, yet never have I seen it turn out like this, someone rendered unconscious. It's possible she has a poor immune system, or there's something else wrong with her. Wait, what am I doing? This is no time to be thinking about these things. I need her to wake up, so I know she's all right.

Still, she looks very pretty as I carry her through the halls.

Her unruly blonde hair, cascading softly across my arm, reminds me of oceanic waves, and my eyes won't leave her cute little mouth. What I wouldn't give to see her smile with her sexy gray eyes lit up. So familiar...

What will she think when she wakes? Will she be as attracted to me as I am to her, or will she blame me for her current condition? She would be right to do so. Damn it, why won't she wake up? I take a deep breath, steadying myself, resisting the urge to shake her awake. The need to protect her is so intense, like never before.

I quicken my pace and arrive at the nurse's office. There, I wait, and even after the nurse tells me to go to my classes, I continue to wait some more. A devastating thought crosses my mind. What if something went wrong with the marking? What if it had some kind of adverse effect on her? What if she never wakes up?

5

AN AWKWARD FIRST MEETING

Marley

Slowly, I open my eyes. I'm lying on a cot in a white room by myself. There's an open cabinet across the room with all kinds of medication bottles, a stethoscope, a blood pressure cuff, and long wooden Q-tips in a jar. I cringe as I look at my surroundings, feeling claustrophobic. I'm at the school nurse's office. I hate doctor's offices, and the nurse's office is much too similar. Lucky for me, I've been here only one other time since I started high school, when I took Becca because she had cramps. I guess I'm lucky when it comes to that department.

Mrs. Brody, the nurse, is outside the room typing on her computer. Why am I here? Think, Marley—what happened? I went to the office to bring the new guy back to Mrs. O'Leary's classroom... Oh crap, I fainted! I cover my face with my hands, embarrassed, even though I'm alone. I'm going to have to face the secretaries in the office again at some point.

I sit up too quickly and have to lie back down. My head is

pounding. I check for lumps but come up with nothing. Well, except that my hair is even more of a mess than before from lying on the cot. I roll on my side, facing the wall, feeling confused, tired, and a little sick to my stomach.

As soon as I can figure out what time it is, I'll know how long I've been here. I push myself up on my elbows, glancing down at the floor. Where's my backpack? I move to get up but stop mid-motion, when I hear a male voice coming from the other room. I cover my mouth with my hand as if they can hear me breathing.

"Hi, Mrs. Brody, I..." It's my friend, Justin Jameson. What's he doing here?

I lean toward the wall as if it will help me to hear him. It's like he forgot what he was going to say. That's not like him at all. Then, after a minute he continues, "I heard Marley fell, and she wasn't in Calc for first period. I have study hall now, and I wanted to make sure she is all right."

"She's resting in the other room. I don't want to wake her, but I believe she will be fine, Justin," Mrs. Brody says. "What a good friend you are to stop by. Now, you should be getting back to study hall."

"Okay, I..." Justin pauses again.

What's going on out there?

"All right, thanks, Mrs. Brody."

I hold my breath as the outer door opens and closes. I exhale, sighing. That was a strange conversation. I stretch my legs out, and my arms over my head, wondering how much longer I have in here before I need to make my wakefulness known.

My thoughts are interrupted by a second, deeper male

voice. "Mrs. Brody, she has to be awake by now, doesn't she? I'd like to make sure she's okay."

My eyes widen as I draw my legs up to my chest, hugging them. There's someone else out there with the nurse!

My head does hurt. Could I have hit it when I fainted? But, if I did, I'd be in a hospital, right? Hospital...the thought is disturbing.

I hear the deep voice again, clearly irritated. "Clearly, she has some kind of medical condition or mental problems. She should not have been sent to the office to get me."

My mouth forms an 'O.' The new boy is here talking to Mrs. Brody! Wait, did he just say mental problems? Oh boy, he probably thinks I fainted because of him! Why, that arrogant son of a... I throw the stiffly-starched sheet and blue thermal blanket aside, swing my legs to the floor, check to make sure I have clothes on, which I do, and stand. I straighten my wrinkled shirt, adjusting my bra as I march over to the door.

Take a deep breath. Mental problems!?!

I throw open the adjoining door and burst into the other room. "Who do you think you are? Coming in here and saying I have mental problems. You probably have mental problems. God, who says that without even knowing a person? It's super rude. I mean, you did surprise me, but that's no reason to question my mental well-being. I also don't have any, what did you call it, a *medical condition* that would prevent me from walking the halls at this school. For your information, I hike five miles at a time on the trails without one false step, and I've fainted only one..." my words trail off as I finally get the courage to look at him instead of the floor, "...other time in my life."

I can't stop staring at him while feeling slightly dizzy again. His dark hair is messy and perfect all at once; clearly, he understands the mechanics of styling products. He's average height, wearing a snug-fitting black t-shirt with faded jeans and... is that a sports coat? It reminds me of a cross between the old shows I sometimes watch late at night, *Miami Vice* and the old *Beverly Hills 90210*. Hmm, I think, arching an eyebrow. Strangely, it works for him.

He shifts his gaze from Mrs. Brody to me, and my head spins a little more. I concentrate on his facial features—tan skin, straight nose, thick arching eyebrows, and full lips. When our eyes finally meet, I realize I didn't imagine the last thing I saw before fainting. His eyes are as black as night.

Oh...and Mrs. Brody is there too, sitting behind her desk. She looks the same as the last time I saw her except maybe a little annoyed.

Shyly, he says, "Ah, I see you're all right."

Well kind of. Wait, why's he being so polite now after what he said? And why would he think there's something wrong with me? I look down to be extra sure. Everything seems to be in order. I look back up. "Yep, I'm fine."

Mrs. Brody looks concerned. "Marley, you're acting very strangely. Do you feel well enough to stay and finish the day?" She nods toward the new boy and continues with a lilt in her voice, a smile on her lips, "You should be thanking your new classmate. He carried you here from the office. Quite gallant, I might add."

Oh...my...GOD! He carried me? I run my hand through my hair nervously. My face feels so hot; it has to be bright red. How embarrassing! I can't look at him again, let alone acknowledge that he carried me!

I stand there unsure of what to do until I realize Mrs. Brody is waiting for a response. "Oh, sorry, I think I was a little shaken up. I'm fine, really. What period is it?"

She smiles. "Oh good. It's third period, and you have about twenty minutes left. Best be on your way, dear."

I turn to the room with the cot, thinking I should get my backpack, only to realize that I left it back in homeroom. When I turn back around to say as much, I realize I'm alone with Mrs. Brody. He's already gone. I open my mouth and shut it. Who is this guy?

* * *

"WHAT HAPPENED TO YOU? Mrs. O'Leary said you had to go to the nurse's office, and you hate the nurse's office," Liz asks as we enter the cafeteria for lunch.

I can see that she doesn't like being left in the dark. I glance down and then back, meeting her concerned eyes. "I collided with the office door. Someone was coming out when I was going in. I hit my head. The nurse wanted to make sure I didn't have a concussion or anything, I'm fine, though." I don't know what's going on yet, but until I do, there's no need to worry Liz.

Liz seems a little wary to accept this. "You ran into the office door?"

I blush and look away.

She seems to reflect on this and smiles slyly. "You should be more careful."

We grab our lunches and park it at our usual table. The conversation moves to our bio exam as Becca starts reviewing her notes with Liz. I drift off, thinking about my encounter with the new boy.

The next thing I know, I sense someone's gaze on me. Liz nudges my arm, her eyes indicating to turn around. My head feels funny, and my face is warming. I know exactly who's standing behind me.

I turn to meet his eyes, and he smiles. His teeth are so white and straight. "Hi, I want to apologize if there was any misunderstanding earlier. I was totally rude to you. My bad. Please accept my apology."

"Forget about it. No big deal."

"My name's William Reed. Most people call me Will. My sister Anna and I moved here from Texas."

Texas? No, that doesn't sound right. "But, you don't have a Southern accent," I respond without thinking.

Liz chimes in, "I think what you meant to say is, 'Nice to meet you, Will. My name's Marley Hunter.'"

Thanks, Liz. I'm amazed that I can have conversations all by myself without her to rein me in.

"Um yeah, sorry...my name's Marley Hunter, but I guess Liz just told you that." I'm stammering, and I can't stop staring at his sports coat. Liz nudges me again.

I blurt, "Oh...*90210.*" I cringe, laughing nervously. I'm such a dork. "What I mean is, this is my friend, Liz Larson, and that's Rebecca Wright, but everyone calls her Becca." This is unbearable. Why am I being such a freak? Now I'm not so sure if he wasn't right earlier in the nurse's office; maybe my mind is scrambled eggs.

Will continues to smile. "*90210?* You mean the TV show?"

"What? I...sorry, I shouldn't have said that." I want to crawl under the table.

Will looks a little confused at my response but recovers quickly. "Well, anyway, it's nice to meet you three. Marley Hunter. What a cool last name... I don't suppose you like to hunt, do you?"

I put on my best fake smile. "Nope, but my stepdad's hunting buddies ask me that all the time." I hate it. I don't dislike hunting *per se*, but I had a terrible experience when I was a kid. I watched a field dressing of a deer. I was eight. The hunter didn't know I was there.

"Oh...sorry. Anyway, you're right about my accent. My family isn't from Texas. We travel quite a bit because of my dad's job. His last position was in Austin, and now it's here." He takes a quick glance around the cafeteria. "I don't want to distract you, so I'll let you get back to studying." Then he's gone.

I open my mouth to say something else, but he's already halfway across the cafeteria. He sits down with a light-haired girl on the far side. I assume that's his sister. When I finally turn back around to face Liz and Becca, they're wearing the biggest grins I've ever seen.

Liz finally speaks. "A door, huh? He's the sexiest door I've ever seen."

MY HEART IS POUNDING by the time I get to my car after eighth period. I had to endure two classes with Will this afternoon, English and Biology. I don't have to sit near him in Biology thanks to my lab partner, Chase, but in English, I could feel him staring at me from across the room. Even though I sit by Justin, I could still sense Will's closeness as if he were right behind me as we began our reading of *Romeo and Juliet*. I'm not that big of a fan of Shakespeare, to begin with, but why couldn't it be *Hamlet*?

Things got worse in eighth period Civics with Mrs. O'Leary when a bunch of us volunteered to do some more trail cleanup tomorrow after school, and I learned that Will also volunteered earlier in the day. Great. After class, I breezed by an open-mouthed Liz and bee lined it to the safety of my car. I couldn't face Liz, not after what happened in the cafeteria. She knows me too well and will have lots to say about our new classmate, Will.

I take a few deep breaths, finally relaxing. It's short-lived, though, because as a school bus pulls away from the curb at the front of the school, I spot a man leaning to one side, hiding behind a tree, looking directly at me. I slink down in my seat, trying to hide but not having anywhere to go. He's tall, wearing a black coat and dark sunglasses. Another bus passes in between us, and he's gone. I pop back up, scanning the parking lot, but there's no sign of him.

Knock it off, Marley. You're being paranoid because of Will. I try to focus back on the very real problem I have. I need to find out why Will is making me feel so strangely. I have to talk to him tomorrow afternoon on the trails. There, I can be brave; I'm perfectly capable of holding an intelligent conversation with a guy who literally makes me weak in the knees. It's going to be fine. I place my shaking hands on the steering wheel.

No, I'm not nervous at all...

6

WINNER TAKES ALL

Will

I can't wait to get out. Sitting behind Marley in the van,
staring at her beautiful bare neck is driving me crazy. My
hand itches to touch her, to trace one of those little blonde
curls that fell down from her ponytail. She senses my presence behind her, too. She's barely spoken to Liz, sitting next
to her, the entire trip.

Finally, we stop at our destination. One by one the ten of
us exit the school van onto the trail, my eyes following the
girl ahead of me. It's a beautiful day, seventy degrees if I'm not
mistaken. High above the paper birch and pine trees is a blue
sky dotted with small white clouds and a western sun.

Mrs. O'Leary bellows over the students' chatter, "All right,
everyone, stay to the northeast of Fuller Lake on the Cumber-
land Trail. That is where most of the cleanup is needed. You
may veer off the trail to secondary trails, but do not veer long.
Considering that our most recent trip involved one of your

classmates getting lost and injured, we will go in pairs from now on."

Thank you, Mrs. O'Leary. I smile and tap Marley on the shoulder. "How about we partner?" I ask, hopeful.

She shifts uncomfortably, glancing at Liz. "Well, I don't want to leave Liz without a partner."

I look from Marley to Liz. "Oh, okay."

"Well..." Liz starts with a mischievous grin, "I actually want to partner with Mrs. O'Leary so we can talk about some of the animals at the shelter. She's all yours, Will."

Marley opens her mouth to respond, but Liz is already sauntering off.

Thank you, Liz. "So then you and I?" I ask, once again hopeful.

"Sure, I guess. But, just so you know, I take the cleanup seriously."

Teasingly, I bump her shoulder with mine. "Of course."

Big mistake. Marley bends down, her hands on her knees, and takes some deep breaths. The effects from the marking are still present.

"Sorry, I've been feeling weird lately," she explains between ragged breaths

Concentrating, I touch her shoulder, easing her discomfort in my special way. "Are you okay?"

Slowly, her breathing returns to normal. She stands, looking better, but suspicious. "How did you do that?"

I shift uncomfortably. I'm not ready for this conversation yet. "Do what?"

"You touched my shoulder, and I felt better. How did you do that?" she asks pointedly, hands on her hips.

I smile confidently. "I don't know what you mean. Maybe

you like me or something." I have to shift the focus back to her.

It works. Her cheeks turn rosy, and she breaks eye contact. "Okay, never mind. Let's get our gear and bags."

Yeah, we better get started. I know what I need to accomplish, and I only have about an hour to do it.

Marley

As we move up the trail, I peer up at him shyly. I can't deny that he's physically fit. He took off his sports coat, revealing a thin white t-shirt that hugs his chest and arms. I guess he wears them every day. I take a deep breath trying to steel my composure. I've never been this affected by someone. I literally get dizzy around him. I mean, despite his boyish grin, he's not my type. He's too stylish. He probably doesn't even like being outside; he's only participating because he's new and wants to fit in. The exertion messes up his hair, I think, smiling to myself.

"What are you thinking?" he asks, catching me mid-thought.

"Nothing," I lie, spotting a granola bar wrapper. I bend to pick it up and deposit it in my garbage bag. Why can't people clean up after themselves? When I stand back up and turn around, he's right in front of me, my face inches below his.

"Listen, I'm sorry if I startled you yesterday. I didn't mean to. I guess it might be difficult to make friends here if your response to me is any indicator."

I smile. He's trying to be nice. I should try too.

"Don't worry about it. It happened, it's over. You know, I might consider being friends, but I don't know if I can keep up with your stylish sports coats," I say jokingly, looking back down at my t-shirt and jeans, starting to get more comfortable.

He laughs. "I'm hurt. You don't like my style then? What would you suggest?"

I swat his arm playfully. "I'm just kidding! Jeez. You can wear whatever you want. Believe me, I'm not exactly a fashion expert, although Liz certainly is. You should ask her."

God, his smile is contagious.

"Yeah, I guess I'll have to do that, but maybe I'll start a new trend here at Pine Grove."

I have no doubt he has that ability, and that's only based on one day at school. I shrug my shoulders and look around for more trash.

I feel his eyes still on me. "Hey, let's make picking up trash a little more interesting. How about a competition?"

I whirl around to face him. "Competition? What kind of competition?"

"A contest. We see who can collect the most trash. Winner gets a prize." He arches one eyebrow enticingly.

"What's the prize?"

"Winner chooses. I know what I want."

"And what's that?"

"Do you have a date for prom yet?"

I'm speechless. Is he the one with mental problems? He doesn't even know me. This is so strange. "Wait," I stammer. "I think I misunderstood you. Are you asking me to go to the prom with you?"

"Only if I win."

I shake my head, feeling seriously confused. "Wait, uh...."
I look back into his eyes, trying to get some kind of read on

him. He looks serious enough; in fact, he seems impatient about my response.

"I'm a little curious about why you would want to take me to the prom. I mean, you barely know me. Seriously, what do you know about me?"

"Oh. Um, awkward..." He shifts his weight from side to side and stares at the ground. "Well, I don't know if you've noticed, but I'm new here, and isn't it customary for new people to try to fit in? As far as what I know about you, you're right, I don't know you that well yet. But, I'd like to get to know you better, and you seem like a nice person. I think we would have fun. Is that too strange?" He looks back up at me, with a hopeful smile. "Besides, I have to win first."

He seems genuine enough, and I don't have a date. "Hmm...I guess I can understand that. It must be hard having to move to a new school in the middle of the year. Okay, well, you're in luck. No one has asked me, so I'm free." Then another thought occurs to me. "Wait, what do I get if I win?"

Will walks toward me slowly, purposefully. He doesn't stop until I can feel his body heat next to mine, forcing me to look up into his eyes. His mirthfulness is gone, replaced by something else, something making my head swim. Steadily, his eyes never leaving mine, he asks, "What do you want?"

My first thought is, *"You!"*

"Uh...I don't know. Can I think about it and tell you if I win?" The butterflies in my stomach won't stop fluttering.

He smiles seductively. "Okay. Here are the rules. We each take a side of the trail, and we meet back here in, say, thirty minutes. Whoever's bag is heavier wins. Sound good?"

"Wait, who determines whose bag is heavier?"

Will chuckles. "Oh, I don't think it'll be that close, but

your friend Liz can decide the winner if you're worried."

I eye him closely. He's serious. He's that sure of himself. "You're pretty confident, aren't you?"

"Yes, yes, I am."

We'll have to see about that confidence when I win. "Okay then, let's do this. You take that side, and I'll take this one." I point to the side by the lake.

He glances down at his wrist. "Okay, set your watch for thirty minutes."

I look down at my black Timex and then back to his wrist. "Let me see that." I grasp his arm. The watch is nice: titanium, timer, a compass, temperature, barometer, and who knows what else.

He smiles. "Well, I think you might have found what your prize should be."

"No, I couldn't. It must have cost a fortune," I say, dropping his arm.

"Not really. Do you like it?"

"Of course. It's an awesome watch." Clearly, his family has quite a bit more money than mine.

"Then it's settled. This is your prize if you win."

Before I can protest, he adds, "Look, you really have no chance of beating me, so you shouldn't worry about how much it costs."

So arrogant! "Okay, you're on." I set my watch. "Ready?"

He nods.

"Go!"

He takes off running, bag in hand. A smile plays at my lips as I think about how pissed he's going be when I win. I move toward the lake, wondering if it's cheating that I got this side of the trail.

＊ ＊ ＊

THIRTY MINUTES LATER, I walk back up to the spot that we agreed on. He's already there, proud as ever, holding a large bag of trash. On one hand, I'm impressed, but on the other, I'm saddened by the fact that there could be this much trash out here.

I bring my half-full bag up to meet him and smile. "Got a big bag there, don't ya?"

"Yep," he says, looking at mine. "I don't really think we need Liz to decide the winner, do you?" He's grinning from ear to ear, clearly thinking he's won.

I give him my best sad, beaten face. "Yeah, I don't think we'll need Liz."

"Prom it is then," he says triumphantly.

I drop my bag and walk back to the trees to grab my other full garbage bag, dragging it back up to where he's standing. "Oh, I don't know about that."

His face is priceless—complete shock and, perhaps, a shade whiter. I double over, unable to control my laughter.

"How did you—"

I interrupt him in between giggles. "It's Fuller Lake, Will. People come here to swim all the time. There's always more trash down by the water because that's where the people are."

When I look back up at him, he's no longer shocked, but gloomy.

"Oh, I'm sorry. I know you thought you would win. It wasn't really a fair contest; you just didn't realize what I already knew. Think of it as home field advantage."

"No, you won, fair and square." He takes off his watch.

I wave him off. "Oh stop it. I'm not taking your watch! You

can buy me lunch at school or something, and...don't be so cocky next time," I reply, smiling.

Will raises his eyes brows, curiously. "Next time?"

"Oh. The outdoors isn't really your thing, huh?"

"Are you kidding? I love it out here. Hiking is like one of my favorite things to do. In fact, I'm very happy my family moved here so I can be close to the trails. I've been a little deprived for a while—Texas was very flat."

"Oh, well you don't have to worry about that here, and spring is one of the best times to hike because the trees are—"

"—so beautiful." His eyes are so intense, and they never leave mine.

The dizziness is back, and I have to look away, but before I do, I swear I see something strange in his left eye.

"Yeah, they are," I reply, shaking my head.

He reaches out and grasps my hand. His gentle stroking feels nice and has a calming effect, as the dizziness subsides.

"Well, we better get back," I say, smiling.

On the walk to the van, Will asks about my family. I tell him about my mom and Ray, which brings up the issue about how my dad died in the military before I was born. It was a little uncomfortable, but the conversation quickly moved on to his family. He was adopted when he was a baby. A year later, his parents adopted his sister, Anna. His dad's job requires them to move around a lot, which has been hard. Oddly, it saddens me to think about him moving away from Pine Grove.

We climb into the van and take our seats; he sits behind me again. Liz is giving me eyes the entire trip back to the school. She's dying to ask me about what happened. She can't, though, since he's sitting right behind us. Occasionally, I turn and smile back at him. He's listening to his iPod, looking out the window. Maybe he's still down about losing. I don't know why, but I have the strangest desire to cheer him up, and I may know just the thing.

The van pulls back into the school parking lot around six. After filing out, we head to the remaining scattered cars in the lot.

Will waves goodbye and turns to head to his car.

"Hey, Will," I say, making him turn back around.

"Yeah?"

"Still want to go to the prom with me?"

His mouth drops open. I've shocked him for the second time today. My heart flutters as I shift my feet uncomfortably.

He's not saying anything.

Okay, this is embarrassing. I should go. I turn around. *Stupid idea.*

"Yes," he says from over my shoulder.

I smile, my hands balling into fists, resisting the urge to jump up and down. Oh my God, what's the matter with me? Quickly, I turn back around and put on my best casual face. "Okay, then, I'll go with you."

His smile, the confident one I saw when we first got off the van this afternoon, is back. "Awesome, see you later." He turns and walks away.

Well, I'm going to the prom. Technically, I think I asked *him*. But, I guess it doesn't really matter. I turn to walk toward my car, too, but notice an open-mouthed Liz, who witnessed the entire exchange.

I reach out and push her chin back up, closing her mouth. "I'll call you later."

7

QUESTIONS

Will

Sorting through Marley's friends has been relatively easy. There's Liz, Marley's best friend since childhood. She's a bit of a fashionista but would walk across hot coals for Marley. Then there's Becca, a girl whose nose is almost always in a book. In fact, that's what she was doing when she fell into the ravine when I first saw Marley. Then, there's Justin. Justin is a loner, and completely in love with Marley. It's so unbelievably obvious to everyone except her. He also seems to have an intense dislike of me. Lastly, Mike Walker and A.J. Morales. Mike dates Liz, and A.J...well, besides his love for football, he's taken a shine to my sister, Anna. A.J. almost hit her in the face with a football in the school parking lot, but she, of course, managed to catch it at the last minute. She can be such a show off sometimes.

Mike, A.J., and I are on the same team today for a basketball game in gym class. I'm not a pro by any means, but I'm very competitive. I hit most of my shots from the three-point line to keep my distance from the other kids. I score the winning shot, and Mike pats me on the back, telling me that I can be on his team anytime. I smile as some of my other teammates compliment me. It's nice to feel normal every once in a while, but it never lasts.

A.J. nods over to the bleachers where there's a group of girls watching the game, smiling and pointing in our direction. I've never had a problem in the girl department, but these girls seem a little over the top. A.J. punches me in the arm and tells me that I can have my pick of them. Even though some of the girls are attractive, none of them are a possibility for me. For one, there's very limited compatibility with my kind, and two, I have my sights on the cute blonde walking into the girls' locker room.

Mike and A.J. follow my line of sight and laugh. Mike says, "Forget it, A.J., Will clearly only has eyes for Marley. Hey, good luck with that, you might need it."

When I ask them what they mean, they tell me that Marley doesn't date anyone. She's only had one boyfriend that they know of, and he was a family friend. In a strange way, I'm satisfied in knowing that she has no interest in anyone else. Mike and A.J. were shocked that Marley is going to the prom with me. Hell, it was a shock to me, too! She bested me at my own game on the trails and then turned around and asked *me* to the prom! God, she's so confusing and surprising, something I'm not used to. One minute she's shy and awkward, and the next she's confident and kicking my ass at a game I thought I had stacked in my favor! I've got to find out more about her.

In that area, I'm making progress. I have plans to take her out on a date soon. It's going to be hard keeping my secret from her for much longer. The prospect of showing Marley my world is so exciting; I can barely wait. After so many tracking assignments, it's refreshing to meet someone I actually connect with.

Earlier today, my sister agreed to go to the prom with A.J. I don't really have a problem with her going, but A.J. better be the model of respect. Anna and I have our fair share of sibling arguments, but she's still my sister. She's insisting I take her to buy a new dress today after school. As if she needs one... She's already got a ton of them. I agreed, but only after I found out that Marley will be dress shopping at the same time and place. Anna is remarkably effective in finding out information. Even if I don't get a chance to talk to Marley after school today, I have plans to see her later after she falls asleep.

Marley

English class. I slide into my seat next to Justin. Ever since he moved here from Alaska two years ago, we've been close. He's quiet with everyone else but never with me. Our friendship started in the cafeteria line when we found ourselves fighting over the last order of pierogies. Incidentally, I won. Today he's wearing his usual tan pants with a white button-down shirt, definitely his mom's choice. His tawny brown hair falls across his forehead, practically covering his blue eyes. But, there's something different about him today. He isn't giving me his usual smile. Instead, he's staring down at his textbook.

"Hey, Justin, how's it going?" I lean toward him, trying to get his attention.

He looks up with the start of a smile. His expression changes to a frown as he notices something behind me. I turn, following his line of sight to see Will coming into the room, taking his seat toward the back. The two eye each other up.

"What's your problem with Will?" I whisper.

Justin focuses back on me. "It's nothing. I just don't like him. There's something strange about him, and I thought I heard him...never mind. He gives me the creeps."

"Hmm..." I glance back at Will, who is pulling his book out of his backpack. "I don't really see the creepiness, Justin. Actually, I kinda like him. He seems really nice," I say cheerfully, hoping to change his mind.

"So, is that why you're going to the prom with him?"

Uh-oh. He isn't asking. He's pissed.

"Listen, Marley, I have a really bad feeling about him. I think you should back out. You can tell him that you changed your mind. If you really want to go to the prom, I could take you."

Okay, now I'm seriously irritated. I hate when people think I can't make decisions for myself. I haven't gotten any bad vibes from Will. In fact, I feel the opposite.

"All right, cut the crap. What's up with you? I'm perfectly capable of running my life and deciding who I want to go the prom with. While I appreciate the fact that you are now asking me to the prom after I've already agreed to go with someone else, I like Will. I'm going to the prom with him. But, I'm not so sure I like you right now. You're kinda being a jerk. So, if you want to stay friends, you'd better start explaining this new attitude to me."

"Forget it. Go to the prom with him. It's your life." Dejected, he looks back down at his book.

I pull my English book from my backpack and slam it down on my desk in frustration.

"Fine," I say sourly.

I look over my shoulder at Will. He raises his eyebrows and hands in the air as if to say, *What? I didn't do anything.* I guess Justin and Will are not going to be friends.

Later in bio, Mr. Bradshaw checks out the little stone I found in my backpack. I haven't been able to show it to him yet. First my lab partner, Chase, stayed after the test on Monday, then we had a substitute for a few days. After everyone leaves, I hold out my hand to show him the stone. He pushes his round wire glasses up on his nose as he studies it.

"Well, isn't that remarkable. May I?" he asks, wanting to hold the stone. I hand it over to him. He turns it over a few times in his palm. "I think this is some type of meteorite. Where did you find it?"

I don't know why, but I have a strong urge to conceal that I found it in my bag. "I was hiking over the weekend and found it on the ground." I hope he doesn't notice what a terrible liar I am.

He holds it up to the light. "You're very lucky to have found this. You see those greenish yellow streaks? They look like some type of fossilized life form. I read an article from about forty or fifty years ago about a stone like this being found in our area. I wonder if they came from the same source. You see right here..." he points to the side of the stone where it isn't smooth, "...it does look like it came from a larger piece."

He's right. I can see how the stone appears to be a part of something larger. "I see what you mean."

He hands the stone back to me. "Give me a minute, I'll go look in my files for that article."

"Okay," I say, never taking my eyes from the stone. It almost feels warmer now back in my palm.

Mr. Bradshaw comes back from his desk with a yellowed newspaper clipping. The article mentions a woman, whose name I don't recognize, hiking the trails and finding a unique stone. There is a picture of the woman smiling, wearing one of those sling things to carry a baby, and I can see a little hand poking out from it. The last thing I notice is the date at the top of the paper: *June 9, 1962.*

"It's very rare to find a specimen like this one. Lucky girl. Keep it someplace safe. Now, I'd better write you a note for being tardy to your next class."

I stuff the stone in my pocket. Lucky? I don't know about that.

8

DRESSY

Marley

I pull into the driveway to find my mom already waiting for me outside. She isn't messing around with this prom dress shopping trip; she means business.

"Hey, Mom," I say, getting out of my car. "I'm ready to go."

"Good. I need some caffeine first. Will you run into Starbucks for me?"

"Sure."

Great, let's go."

Ten minutes later, I'm waiting for my mom's iced coffee and my strawberry smoothie at the Starbucks counter.

A middle-aged man with long dark hair wearing a suit and dark sunglasses hanging from the front of his a-little-too-open button-up shirt approaches me. There's something about his smile that I don't trust. "Excuse me, Miss, but did you drop this?"

I glance down at his outreached hand and gasp. It's an onyx stone just like the one I found. Quickly, I check my pockets. It's not there. It must have fallen out when I paid for the drinks. *Really careless!* I reach for the stone. "Um, yeah, thanks."

Before I can pull away, he grasps my hand with his other one, holding the stone between us. "You have such interesting eyes."

The hair on the back of neck stands on end. My instinct is to pull away, but I can't. I want my stone back. "Uh, thanks," I reply, tensely.

Let go of me!

"Double espresso for Malcolm," a tall, thin male barista says, placing a cup on the counter next to us.

The man releases me. "Well, that's me," he says, picking up the cup. "Have a nice afternoon. Oh, and I'd put that stone someplace safe. It looks to be valuable."

I smile weakly and nod.

After he leaves, I pocket the stone and start breathing again. What a creep...

MY MOM PULLS into Madeira's dress shop a half an hour later, and I still have the heebie-jeebies from the man at the coffee shop. But, there's no sense in dwelling now. There's shopping to be done. When we walk inside, I'm amazed at the large selection and realize it's going to take a while to get through all these dresses.

I recognize a few girls from school, but there's one girl who looks familiar, but I can't place her. I'm not sure if she even goes to Pine Grove High, which is entirely possible because both Greencastle and Shippensburg have proms, as well. She's beautiful with a slight build, short blonde hair, and vibrant angled light blue eyes. She reminds me of Tinker Bell. When she turns, our eyes meet, and she smiles. The cafeteria at school. That's where I saw her. Before I know it, she's standing in front of me.

"You must be Marley. Hi, I'm Anna, Will's sister. I recognize you from your picture in the yearbook. My brother pointed you out yesterday. He said he's taking you to the prom." She pauses, giving me an up and down.

I blush, looking away from her gaze. So uncomfortable.

"Well, he's got good taste. You're pretty. Would you mind if we shop together? I have absolutely no idea what to pick. A.J. Morales invited me to your prom. I guess because I'm new, and he didn't have a date already." She's speaking a mile-a-minute; it's hard to keep up.

I smile at her. "Wow, you talk fast!"

We both laugh.

"It's nice to meet you," I continue, feeling a little self-conscious by her strange familiarity with me and her offer to shop together. "So, you're going with A.J.? You must really like football." I can see with my own eyes why he asked her, but, honestly, does the poor girl know what she's getting into?

Anna looks confused. "Football? Well, I suppose it's okay. Why do you ask?"

Oh, that's right. She just met him. Well, who am I to give advice? They might be perfect for each other. "Oh, no reason, I know that he's hoping to get a scholarship to Penn State for football."

Her smile returns. "Oh, yeah, he did tell me that."

I point over to the woman with at least ten dresses already draped over her arm. "That's my mom, Susan."

Anna waves and calls over to her, "Nice to meet you!"

My mom smiles back at her, waving.

Oh no, not again. I reach up to rub my forehead. My head feels funny, like I'm in a cloud of steam, and I can't get out. It's the same as before, and I know what Anna is going to say next.

"My brother's outside if you want to say hello. He drove me here to shop. I guess coming inside a dress shop would ruin his image," she says, her attention outside the shop. When she turns back, she can tell I'm not feeling well. "Hey, are you okay?"

"Yeah, it'll pass. I've had some dizzy spells lately," I reply quietly, not wanting my mom to see me. She'll fuss.

"There are some chairs over there if you need to sit down—"

Will is by my side before Anna can finish, holding me by the arm. "Marley, are you okay? I saw you from outside, and you look sick."

As soon as he touches me, the spinning stops, and I relax. This response to him is driving me crazy. Maybe there really is something wrong with me.

"I'm fine." I take a step away from him and look around for my mom, adding quietly, "Don't make a big deal out of this." Thankfully, she must have gone to the back of the store. The last thing I need is my mom freaking out.

"Oh, okay, well, I wanted to be sure," he says, glancing out the window.

How odd. Why isn't he looking at me? "I'm fine, really." I tilt my head, trying to get him to look at me. *Hello?*

Anna says, "Will, unless you want to help us shop for dresses, you should go."

"Oh, yeah, okay. You two have fun," Will says uncomfortably, still not making eye contact.

Then he's gone.

"My brother's so weird sometimes, but I guess it's because..." Anna stops mid-sentence and changes the subject. "Okay then, want to shop?"

I gaze outside the dress shop at Will. Why wouldn't he look at me? It can't be because he's shy. Embarrassed?

Anna links her arm with mine, pulling gently, trying to coax me back into shopping. "There are a ton of dresses. We better get started."

"Yeah, okay." I allow her to pull me along, not ready to take my eyes away from the dark-haired boy outside the shop.

We scout out the entire place and end up with five dresses each. Two of my five are ones my mom picked out. Anna and I each try on our selections one by one, modeling them. The last time I wore a dress this formal was at my mom and Ray's wedding. I'm not really the dress up kind of girl. It seems so impractical anyway. What's worse, I don't even know what looks good and what doesn't. For that, I'm thankful my mom and Anna are here to help. It's a little weird modeling the dresses, but at least I'll get honesty from my mom. So far she simply shook her head to two of them because they were too short, and gave me a 'meh' to two more. However, Anna said I looked nice in all of them.

I put on the last dress, the one that seems a little too old fashioned, and spin in front of the mirror. Not bad. It's a long strapless dark purple gown embroidered with lace and little lavender flowers sewn at the top. The flowers hide the fact that I don't have much going on in that department. I nod at myself in the mirror approvingly.

I walk out to model, and it's an instant hit. Anna tells me that the dress complements my eyes. I didn't realize that any color could complement gray eyes, but apparently that color is purple. My mom beams with satisfaction. Of course, it's one of the dresses she picked out.

Anna ends up with a shorter light pink dress with spaghetti straps that complements her light skin tone and light blonde hair. She looked beautiful in all the dresses she tried on, but the pink one is perfect.

I take one last look at my prom dress before they place it in a bag—beautiful. I can barely contain the smile on my face or the pangs of excitement in my belly. I'm really going to the prom. Embarrassed by my own giddiness, I walk back toward the dressing rooms to hide.

Don't do a happy dance. Calm down. It's no big deal. Lots of girls go to the prom. I take a deep breath, feeling a bit calmer. It's short-lived, though, because the next thing I know I'm being shoved head first into a big rack of dresses. The rack topples and comes crashing down on top of me.

"Hey!" I yell, clawing at the mound of dresses now covering my face. "What the hell?"

"Oh my God, Marley! What happened?" Anna yells, pulling dresses aside and searching for my arms.

"What? I don't know. Someone pushed me. Didn't you see them?"

Anna grabs my hand and pulls me to my feet, leaving a pool of dresses around my ankles. Checking myself, I discover that my hair is a mess, and my right arm is a little sore.

Anna looks around the store, not responding.

"Hello? Anna?"

Finally, she turns back to me. "I'm sorry, Marley. I didn't see anyone."

"Okay, well, this is really weird. Why would someone push me like that?" Could Anna have done it?

Then my mom comes over. "Marley, did you make this mess?" Before I can answer she continues, "Well, you better get started cleaning it up. I need to get home to make dinner."

I open my mouth to tell her someone pushed me, but it doesn't matter. I'm still going to have to clean up the dresses. I shrug my shoulders, resigned, and pick up an empty hanger from the floor, eyeing Anna cautiously. She rights the clothing rack and hands me a dress. Well, either Anna wanted the dress I picked or someone out there really doesn't like me.

9

SAILING

Will

W hat happened in there?" I ask Anna, who's leaning nonchalantly against the brick exterior of the dress shop. I'm not feeling so casual. In fact, I'm pissed. As annoying as it would have been, I should have helped the girls shop.

"Back off, Will. I don't know," Anna replies, pushing me out of her personal space. "One minute everything was great, and the next Marley is on the ground covered in dresses." Anna tries, unsuccessfully, to hide her mischievous smile.

My eyes bore into hers, my expression unchanged. "It's not funny, Anna. Let's cut to the chase. Did you do it?"

Anna's frowns and her eyes turn serious at my accusation. "It wasn't me, Will, I promise. I sensed another one of us close by, but when I scanned the shop, I couldn't find a trace. You believe me, right? I didn't push her, I swear."

"Fine. But listen, we have to be extremely careful from here on out with Marley. If someone else is close by, you know what that could mean. Now, Mom isn't with us..." I shift uncomfortably, thinking about my last assignment.

"So what are you saying? You don't think Malcolm is around, do you? He wouldn't take that risk after what happened, would he?"

"No, I don't think so. But, who knows with him? I don't want to take any chances."

"Okay, well, Parker West is in town to see Dr. Arcanas for his son, right? He'll help us, and you have me."

I run my hand through my hair and look up at the sky, feeling intensely stressed. What is happening to me? I've done this dozens of times. "I can't lose her."

"You won't."

I swallow hard and nod. Man, I really need to get back on my game. I don't know what it is, but Marley is constantly making my head swim.

The next thing I know, Anna hits me in the arm, harder than she probably needed to, making me scowl. "Now snap out of this sappy crap and let's go home." She turns and walks over to my car.

Rubbing my arm, I follow her. She's right. The sooner we get home, the sooner I can go to sleep and see Marley. It's time to speed things up.

Marley

That night, I have another dream.

I'm standing in a hallway at school, wearing the same eyelet white shirt and jeans, when I sense a presence behind me. I spin around to find Will wearing his usual sports coat, t-shirt, and jeans. There are lights coming from his eyes, like spotlights, strangely beautiful. The closer he moves toward me, the more clearly I see his eyes. They are their usual black, but tiny green specks floating around in his irises remind me of glowing fireflies at dusk.

"Marley, I don't mean to frighten you. I was hoping to take a walk," he says as he reaches his hand out to me.

"What's going on with your eyes? They look so strange."

He smiles. "My eyes change from time to time," he says, dismissing my question. "So, how about that walk?"

"Okay, I guess." My eyes never leave his, but I take his hand.

"You know, you're so interesting, Marley."

Me? Interesting? "Why? What's so interesting about me? I'm actually kinda boring. I'm the girl who prefers ponytails, hikes, and getting good grades. Isn't that the definition of dorky?"

Will shakes his head in disbelief, but his smile never leaves his lips. "Well, first of all, I like the outdoors too. I don't know if you could ever like it as much as me, but still, it's surprising. Most girls aren't into that sort of thing. Also, you kicked my ass at picking up trash on the trails. I'm very competitive, yet you completely blind-sided me. That *never* happens. Then to top it all off, you asked *me* to the prom. Every time I turn around you surprise me and...well, confuse me. I guess it makes me want to get to know you better."

"Well, I don't know about all that. I do love to hike. It's something I've always been passionate about. Now if only I could major in that in college."

He laughs.

"As far as your little competition on the trail goes, you were being really cocky, which is why I felt it was my personal responsibility to beat you," I say, arching a brow challengingly.

He nods and shrugs his shoulders, looking everywhere but at me. "I guess I can be a little too competitive."

It's a concession. I'll give him that. "Yeah, well, I guess I can kind of understand that. I'm pretty confident about my abilities in hiking and climbing too."

He smiles, and my skin tingles in that melty sort of way.

"I don't know what it is about you, but I understand what you mean about confusing. You make my head spin sometimes, but then you also make me better. I want to know how you do that."

A mischievous smile plays at his lips. "Maybe we share a special connection."

"Maybe..." I reply, still not sure I want to leave it at that.

We walk a bit further, holding hands in silence. Abruptly, he stops and turns toward me. "Hey, you want to do something fun? I can do lots of cool things here. Have you ever been sailing?"

"No, I haven't. But isn't this a dream? What do you mean you can do cool things here?"

"Come on, don't be afraid. It'll be so much fun." His eyes glow more vibrantly.

I open my mouth to ask about his eyes again when he pulls me against his chest. "Shut your eyes," he whispers against my hair.

I obey, unsure what else to do this close to him, feeling his heart beating against my cheek. When I finally open my eyes, we're on a small sailboat in the middle of the ocean. It's jarring, having such a drastic change of scenery. My eyes slowly adjust to the light, and I take in the view. Breathtaking.

The sun is setting over the horizon, leaving only a sliver of bright light across the sea. I can't help but gasp, smiling, still in his arms.

"I thought you might like it. It's great, right?" Enthusiasm brews in his voice. Not allowing me out of his grasp, he adds, "If you look over there, you'll see a small private island. It's so small, in fact, that almost no one knows about it. We can go there sometime, if you like."

I can't explain it, but I love feeling close to him. It's like nothing I've ever felt before, almost like something inside me craves to be near him. He releases me to tighten and loosen things around the boat. I try to get myself under control. I'm getting a little too hot and bothered. This is a dream, right? He's not really here, right? I look back at the island and realize something, something important.

I don't know this place. How am I dreaming about something that he knows?

The hair on the back of my neck prickles. This isn't right. He's watching me. "Please don't go," he says, touching my arm.

His hand is so hot I flinch and move my arm away. He turns away from me, and it's as if I hear his thoughts. *She's not ready. She needs more time.*

I need more time? What's he talking about? This isn't right. I don't want to be here anymore. My breathing quickens.

When he turns back around, his eyes are so bright with light, it's blinding.

I shut my eyes.

I sit up in my bed, waking with a start. I've always had vivid dreams, but this is getting out of hand. This dream was not like some of the other dreams I've had about Will, dreams that I know are mine. I blush in the darkness, thinking about how personal and intimate those dreams were. But this is different. This is the second *real* dream I've had about him. I understand why I'm dreaming about him, but why are they so real? His eyes. They were glowing, with little fluorescent fireflies, so familiar to me. Inadvertently, I touch my shoulder. They're the same as the spots that were left on my shoulder during the episode I had in the ravine.

I fall back, letting my hair splay around me on the pillow, staring up at the ceiling. I've thought about telling him that I had a strange dream, and he was in it, but it might sound weird. I grasp another pillow and press it down on top of my face, smothering myself, groaning. What makes me even more pathetic is that I can't wait to fall back asleep and dream about him some more...

It's Friday afternoon, and Will is planning to come over tonight to meet my parents. We are going out to dinner afterward. I hope that my parents like him. What could go wrong, really? He dresses nicely, and he's very respectful of all the teachers at school. I'm sure he'll be perfect with my mom and Ray too. Still, I'm nervous about it. Should I wear some makeup? I'm so not good at dating.

Making matters worse is the fact that Liz has been on my back constantly about him. "Marley, I'm telling you, there's something special about that guy. You can sense his presence before he even walks in a room. How exciting is that?" Then she looks off, all dreamy-like. She doesn't know the half of how he affects me.

I duck out of homeroom as soon as the final bell rings, heading to my car, needing a moment to myself before I face my parents and Will in the same room. I ease into the driver's seat, relaxing my shoulders.

My mind swims with a thousand thoughts about my reaction to Will. I try to relax and stop thinking, but I can't. Will's eyes...the stone in my bag...oh my God! I bolt upright with a revelation. I grab my backpack and search for the stone. It's at the bottom with my pencils and pens. I hold it in my hand, feeling its smoothness and warmth, the streaks of green striking on the black onyx. I close my eyes, and picture Will's eyes from my dreams. Who is he? What's the connection between the Will I see at school and the one in my dreams? I know it's the same person, but what are those tiny fireflies in his eyes? I look down, turning the stone over and over in my hand, so soothing. I close my eyes, relaxing back against my seat.

I sense a presence. Someone is staring at me. It's the same feeling I had in the ravine. My eyes fly open, and Will is there, standing beside my car, barely moving, his eyes intent. The little fireflies are there, just like in my dreams. I can't move; my lips part in awe. I have no clue what's going to happen, but I'm pretty sure it's going to alter my life forever.

10

TUMBLING RUN

Marley

I consider locking the door, but instead I roll down my window. "Hey, are you wearing contacts?"

Will grabs the door handle and opens my car door.

"What are you—"

"I'll drive, if you don't mind." He scoots me to the passenger seat, not an easy task considering there's a stick shifter and emergency brake in the way.

"Hey, wait a second, I do mind! This is *my* car! Get out right now!" My temper flares as I hit and push him.

He reaches over and grabs my hands. "Listen, I think we need to have a conversation, just the two of us. I know you have questions, and I may have some answers, but you are new to driving a manual, and I'm an expert, in comparison. Right now, I need to get out of here as quickly as possible before someone else notices my eyes."

I stop fighting, dumbfounded, unable to reply. How does

he know I'm new to stick? And where are we going? I hope he's not planning to...

I glance up at him. No, he wouldn't hurt me. At least I don't think so. Oh shit, I'm so freaking out.

He starts the car, throws it in reverse, and we're out of the parking lot in less than a hot minute.

"Would you please stop holding my stone so tightly? It's getting uncomfortable."

Uncomfortable? I look down at my hand to realize I'm still holding the stone. "Why would that make you—"

"I know it sounds strange. I promise I'll explain everything to you, but not now. In the meantime, can you please put it down or something?"

I release my grip. I was holding the stone so tightly that it left indentations on my palm. Quickly, I set the stone down in the center console, and Will sighs in relief. "Sorry. My mom tells me that I clench my fists when I'm nervous."

Will, obviously recovered, smiles at me for the first time since he entered my car. "Do I make you nervous?"

Heat rises to my cheeks. Damn it. Why does he have this effect on me? "Well, of course I'm nervous. You're stealing my car, you're kidnapping me, and you're being all weird about a stone." I look out the side window, unable to face him. "Where are we going anyway?"

I feel his eyes on me. "We're not strangers, you and I. We've been spending lots of time together in our dreams."

My head snaps back toward him. "Dreams?" How can he know about my dreams? Is nothing private? "How?" I fumble, unable to find the words. How can Will possibly know what I dream about at night? Oh my God, what other things does he know?

He seems to sense my fear and rests his hand on mine. "I swear, I'll tell you everything, but right now I need to concentrate on the road." He moves his hand back to the stick shift, throws it into fifth, and takes off down the highway by our school. "You're making it quite difficult, by the way."

He's grinning again.

"Good," I respond, turning my attention back out the passenger window.

Silence.

Okay, well apparently we're not going to talk for the remainder of the car ride to who knows where. I rest my hands on my thighs, trying to pull myself together, nervous about what he has to tell me and creeped out by the fact that he knows what I dream about. Those specks in his eyes are certainly like nothing I've ever seen before. I glance at him slyly. He's wearing his usual t-shirt and sports coat with jeans. I feel an incredible pull to him, and it's not his boyish grin that's got me bothered...it's...something else. I don't know who or what he is, but I'm pretty sure I'm about to find out.

I recognize the area as we head into the mountains, the telltale swerves and gradual uphill slope of the road. It's a familiar climb, my stomach tossing and turning with each tap on the brakes. Will pulls into the parking lot at Tumbling Run, one of my favorite trails. He turns off the car and reaches for my hand. "Do you trust me?"

I have absolutely no reason to trust him. Not one single reason. I should get out of this car right now and flag someone down. I could tell them, "Help me. There is this crazy guy who kidnapped me." In truth, Will has taken over my car, my person, my dreams, and God knows what else.

This is nuts. It's insane. I should *not* trust him. A voice in my head tells me what to say. He's waiting for a response...

I take a deep breath and put my hand in his. "Absolutely."

He smiles.

We get out of the car and walk over the bridge to the beginnings of the trickling stream. I've been here a bunch of times with Liz, and also with my stepdad, Ray. This particular trail is a part of the Appalachians, about a two-mile hike upward. The coolest part is that as you walk up, you have to maneuver around and over a stream that flows downward. At one point, there is a five- to six-foot drop of water that pools on a large ledge of the trail, hence the name, Tumbling Run. Sometimes hikers strip off their hiking gear and hang out in the pool on the ledge. It's quite refreshing in the heat of summer. However, since it's April, and the temperature today is only about sixty degrees, I don't really feel like a swim.

We're about a quarter of a mile up the trail when Will stops me. The pool is about another hundred feet further up. There are no other hikers today. We're completely alone. Waves of fear and anticipation at our solitude wash over me. We stand there for a few minutes, catching our breath and taking in our surroundings. I close my eyes, breathing in the smell of pine and fresh water, trying to glean some comfort from the familiar scents. Glancing down, I see that my shoes are covered with dirt. Luckily I wore jeans and sneakers to school today. A loud squawk above us echoes in my ears. I look up in the sky to see a hawk gliding past.

Will finally turns to me. "How are you feeling?"

It takes me a second to realize he's talking to me because my mind is wandering. "I'm okay. Sometimes I still feel tiny tremors, and my head hurts when I'm near you, or you touch me. Other times, you make me feel better. The dizziness goes away almost instantly. For now, I'm better than when we were in the car. You know, I think it also has something to do with being out here on the trail. I've always felt comfortable out here." I'm rambling because I'm nervous. I look down, kick at a rock on the trail, and watch it tumble into the water. "Okay, now I sound kind of dumb because you never acknowledge the effect you have on me."

Will takes my hand and turns me toward him, the little lights in his eyes swirling around as if energized. "There's nothing dumb about how you feel. It's my chondria that relax you. Unfortunately, while they're comforting you, they're unsettling me. You have no idea how much. I think it's time I do some explaining."

My eyebrows knit together, thinking hard. What's he talking about? Chondria? Is that what I can see in his eyes? This is getting weird. "Okay, wait a second. I'm not so sure I want to know. I mean, you aren't going to tell me something horrible, are you? Like you're a demon or something, here to steal my soul? You should know, I don't really believe in any of that. If that's the case and you're some insane person, I *really* don't want to know." I take some deep breaths, trying to stifle the panic rising in the pit of my stomach.

Will looks taken aback at first, then he doubles over in a fit of laughter.

I walk over to him and hit him in the arm for the second time today. "Okay, haha! I'm pretty funny, huh? I'm not the one with lights in their eyes!"

He finally rights himself and grabs my hand. "I'm sorry to laugh, it's just, I didn't expect you to say something like that." His serious demeanor returns. "I promise you, I'm not a demon, and no, I don't think what I have to say is horrible. I hope you don't think it is either, but look, if you don't want to talk about what's going on with us, we don't have to."

I'm still really uneasy, but my gut tells me to give him the benefit of the doubt. "Okay, I guess. Start explaining, because I'm about to freak out."

Will searches my eyes, and then sighs. "Are you scared of me? Please don't be. I would never hurt you. It's that...ah, I don't want you to worry. You twist your face up like that when you're anxious or scared. I thought that if we came out here where you are most comfortable, it would be best."

I open my mouth to ask when he's seen me scared before but think better of it.

Will looks up at the waterfall. "I want to try something, but it will only work if you are calm. My chondria can help you relax. Maybe you should lie down." He takes off his jacket, revealing a black t-shirt, and spreads it out on the grass in front of me.

I start backing up. He's got to be kidding, right? I look directly at him. "Wait, you want me to lie down?"

He nods and smiles. "Well, yeah."

Oh no you didn't. "Okay, I see where this is going. I don't know exactly what you have planned, but if you think I'm going to let you do some weird physical thing to me, you are mistaken. You may be hot, and up until you kidnapped me, I was kind of into you, but I'm not that kind of girl. I mean, we haven't even been on one date yet," I say, articulating perfectly, so there's no misunderstanding.

He smirks and crosses his arms casually. "Wait, hang on, you think I'm hot?"

I throw my hands up in the air, exasperated. "You're

kidding me, right? I mean...uh, yeah, there are elements about you, you know, that are *hot*," I whisper the word 'hot' as if it were a secret, but really, I'm just embarrassed by my confession. "Besides, I think you know perfectly well that most of the girls at school find

you— "

"Bangable?" he asks, nonchalantly, then rolls his eyes. "Yeah, I heard."

I gasp and cover my mouth. Did he just say what I think he did? I narrow my eyes at him. "Let's cut to the chase. What exactly do you think I'm going to let you do to me? I'm *not* having sex with you. So if that's what your intent is, you can forget it."

Will's demeanor changes back to serious. "Hold on, Marley. You've totally misunderstood. I would never do anything so disrespectful. Besides, I'm required to live a somewhat honorable lifestyle and would never disgrace my family, or yours, like that. I do have parents who taught me right from wrong just like everyone else." He pauses and I can see his frustration building. "My God, do you really think I could do something like that? I mean, what kind of a person do you think I am?" He takes one last glance at me and turns away.

Honorable lifestyle? Required? This is totally weird. I look down at my feet, not sure what to do at this point. I don't want to offend him, but obviously, I already have. I shouldn't have assumed he was trying to sex me up. Now I feel stupid and presumptuous. I'm about to say as much when he turns back around, looking calmer. My voice sticks in my throat as a moment of silence settles around us, leaving only the sounds of the waterfall.

Finally, he says, "I shouldn't have teased you. I'm sorry. All I meant to do was make you more comfortable so that we could talk."

Just talk? Hmm... "Okay, well what do you mean by comfortable? Why would I need to be—"

"So that you don't get freaked out when you realize I'm not talking to you using my voice."

"Wait, I don't..." I stop, trying to process what's happening. He said something to me, but I didn't hear him out loud. His mouth didn't move at all when he spoke. How did he do that? I rack my brain for some type of explanation. Wait a second, I remember seeing a special on PBS about how we only use a small portion of our brain, and that we have no idea what the rest of our brains are capable of. But then I also heard that was a myth. Has Will tapped into a part of his brain that most of us have not? Mind control? Mind reading? *Can you hear me right now? Hello?*

Will's smile returns. *"If you think that I can read your thoughts, you would be wrong. I can only receive messages from others who have chondria, and only if they choose to do so. Also, I can't control your mind in any way; your actions and private thoughts are your own. I can simply talk to you without making a sound,"* he thinks into my mind.

Wow, this is crazy. How's it possible for him to do this? His rich, deep voice sounds as clear and normal in my head as it does when he speaks aloud. In a strange way, it reminds me of listening to my iPod, almost like his voice is already inside my head.

"Do it again," I request with an edge of child-like excitement mixed with fear.

Will smiles and thinks, *"You're a very strange girl, Marley. Why do I feel like I'm a bear in a circus?"*

The voice sounds the same as before. "So, you can talk to me with your mind, and then I can respond out loud?"

He nods.

It occurs to me that this isn't really happening, and I might be hallucinating. "So, is this for real? Who are you? How are you able to do this?" I'm not sure if the answer will frighten me, or make me like him less, but I need to know.

Will sits down and slowly leans back against a rock. He motions for me to do the same. I sit down on his coat, careful not to put my shoes on it, and lean back, as well. I turn to face him, expectantly. Please let it be a simple explanation, something about him being smart and using more of his brain. Please don't let him be crazy. I can't do crazy. Please, please...

"Well, for starters, I'm not entirely human."

All right, we're going with 'crazy town.' *Check, please.* I'm up, again, running back down the trail.

11

CHONDRIA

Will

It takes me a few seconds to register what's happening. Marley's bolting. I scramble to my feet and take off after her. "Marley! Wait, you don't understand!"

"Stay away from me!" she yells, turning her head, her hair waving in the wind like a banner. The effort makes her stumble, giving me just enough time to catch up as she teeters over some tree roots. I grasp her arm and pull her back, holding her to my chest.

"Let me go! You're crazy!" She struggles desperately in my arms. If I let her go, she will take off running again. I have to make her see that she doesn't need to be afraid. Certainly, the fight or flight instinct will pass.

"Marley, please calm down. I'm sorry. I shouldn't have been so blunt." I press my face into her hair, trying to calm her. She stops moving. God, she smells amazing! Vanilla and apples. My head floats as her scent intoxicates me. Why does she have this effect on me?

Her loud voice reminds me of our current situation. "Let me go!" Then she's struggling to get free again.

I loosen my grip on her. "Please calm down first."

She relaxes, and we stand there for a moment. She's weighing her options. I'm stronger than her, but hopefully, she also knows that I would never, could never, hurt her. She needs to calm down and think clearly. If I can make her see that I'm not a threat...

Marley stomps down hard on my foot and elbows me in the stomach, causing me to let go of her.

I double over; she's knocked the wind from my lungs. I croak quietly, "Wait—"

She turns and takes off back down the trail, stopping when there are about twenty feet of distance between us. She turns and looks back up at me, both fear and concern written on her face. "You can't just grab a person like that! God!"

I catch my breath and stand. "Please, don't go. I promise I won't hurt you."

"Before I let you anywhere near me, tell me what all this is about? Are drugs involved? More importantly, have you been drugging me? Is that why I feel strange around you? Just tell me the truth."

Focus. I've been in this situation tons of times. It should be autopilot. I should be confident, no doubts about my abilities. But, instead, I'm shaking with a fear of something I've never felt before. I'm afraid of losing *her,* and not just her viable body. "I swear there are no drugs involved, and I'm not crazy." I start to move toward her, and with each step I take, she takes one back.

"Stay where you are."

I freeze and put my hands up in surrender. "Okay, I won't move. But promise me you won't run off again." I hold my breath, waiting for her response, knowing it will either save or shatter me.

"I won't run. Just give me a minute to catch my breath, and just...just stay there." She bends down, her head forward, hands on her knees, trying to catch her breath.

I exhale. She's willing to hear me out. "I can help you—"

She glances back up at me and drops to her knees on the ground. "No...stay...there."

She's really winded. Ignoring her request to keep my distance, I stride down to her. I reach out my hand to touch her, and she flinches.

My heart goes into my stomach. She doesn't trust me. She thinks I'm a threat. I withdraw my hand and run it through my hair. Damn it, what am I going to do now? Let her go? I would never hurt her. How can she possibly think I ever would? I drop down on my knees in front of her. "I swear to you, on my life, I would never, ever want to hurt you. Please believe me and hear me out."

She looks up at me, her breathing slowly returning to normal, and her gray eyes are filled with tears. "All right, you've got one shot at this, Will, so you better make it good. If I don't like what you have to say, I'm outta here. We clear?"

"Crystal."

"So you're...you're not human? What does that even mean?"

"Okay, I'll admit, it probably wasn't the best opener. But, it's not what you think." I take a chance and grasp her hand, desperately hoping that she might listen to what I have to say.

"Please don't be scared, Marley. I promise you there is nothing to be afraid of. If you let me, I want to tell you about what you see in my eyes, and how I'm different from you."

She's considering it. Her eyes tell me that she's vacillating back and forth. She wants to trust me. I know it. She takes a deep breath. "Okay, but can you promise me that your plan isn't to kill me or anything?"

"Oh my God, of course not. Do you really think I'm capable of something so horrible?"

She studies me, and I know she's not looking at my eyes, but what she sees *in* my eyes. I hold my breath, unable to still my nerves.

"I have no reason to, but I believe you."

I sigh, relieved. "Thank God." Standing, I pull her up with me. "Are you sure you're okay, now?"

"I think so."

"Go back up to our spot?" I ask, hopefully.

She smiles, cutting the tension. "Okay, but no funny business, Mr. Not Entirely Human." She's making light of the situation, but I can tell she's still serious.

I relax. "I promise. If you want any funny business, it's entirely up to you."

She swats at me with a half-smile, and I know we're going to be okay.

We make our way back up the trail to my jacket and sit back down. Marley draws her legs underneath her, turning toward me expectantly. The hardest part is over, but there is so much more to tell her.

"Do you mind if I think to you instead of talking out loud? I've been dying to think to you for a while."

"A while, huh? Okay." She's curious. That's a good thing.

"*Thanks. The first thing I remember in my life is my mom. She told me that she found me in an orphanage when I was a baby. She knew I needed her, so she adopted me and raised me as her own. I attended regular schools, but we moved around a lot. When I was younger, I had some difficulty controlling my chondria. Someone would see my eyes light up, and we had to move right away. My mom was also my teacher in that respect, teaching me how to bond and relate with chondria. I suppose you're wondering what chondria are?*"

"Your eyes, right? They are, what did you call them... chondria? So are they little parasites or something?" She's completely transfixed, obviously eager to learn more.

"*Not exactly, let me explain. Okay, well, so this next part will sound a little strange, partly because you may not understand, but also because it isn't really my story to tell. Before my mom came for me at the orphanage, she had been hiking in the Appalachians, not far from here actually. My mom discovered a covered, untraveled area that led to a secluded enclosure surrounded by trees. In that enclosure, she found what she called a large meteorite. Inside, my mom discovered brightly lit organisms like you see in my eyes now.*

"*They are some kind of life form, not of this world, Marley. We have no idea where they came from or why they came here. There are theories of course, but nothing concrete, at least not yet. The only thing we are sure of is that they are intelligent. We decided to call them chondria because they reminded us of mitochondria in single cells, powerhouses that convert energy into something quite extraordinary. Once chondria bond with a human's DNA, they allow that person to tap into parts of the brain that were dormant, previously. Chondria assist us in other areas, as well. For example, my talking to you with thoughts right now is impressive, isn't it?"*

The waterfall, trickling water bouncing off one mossy rock to the next, captivates her. She's processing what I've told her. A slight turn of her mouth indicates fascination and wonderment. That's a good sign. She looks back at me and quickly realizes I asked her something. "Oh, sorry. I was just thinking about what that must have been like for your mom. So, what else can you do?" She's looking more at ease, and her breathing is normal.

I relax against the rock, my body releasing its tension. Instinctually, I put my arm around her. This time, she doesn't flinch, but instead, leans into me. "All in good time," I say aloud and smile.

"My mom has little to no memory of how chondria bonded with her that day, so we don't know how that first union occurred. However, we do know that chondria thrive inside hosts as I have explained. I don't really remember my bonding as I was so young, but it can be different for each host. For some hosts, it feels strange, for others it is euphoric, and still for others, it can be painful. My mom, luckily, was a compatible host. This is an important detail that I can't stress enough. There are very few, and I mean very few human beings, who are compatible with chondria. My belief is that my mom simply got lucky. If you ask her, she believes that she was destined to find them.

"After she bonded with chondria, she felt incredible and had an overwhelming urge to find other potential hosts. It took some time to find others who were compatible, but she found me first. You see, chondria can help to find other potential hosts, but there is more to it than that. It's not an exact science. We can sense the presence of

another potential host, but it is only a guide to a general location. It is sometimes difficult to make sure we are correct. That is also why my mom knew she would need help. We found that together we stood a better chance at finding hosts.

"At this point, there are a few hundred 'host families' around the world. It has been a long journey but worth it. As far as we know, being a host does not hurt a human in any way. In fact, it makes the person stronger and saves an intelligent life form that would have otherwise been extinct."

I smile down at her. She opens her mouth to ask a question, but I interrupt her, forgetting that I haven't told her the most important and serious piece of information for a potential recruit.

"Please understand, though, no human being should ever be forced into being a host. There should always be a choice as it would not be a positive union if there were any force involved. Even though my mom doesn't remember her bonding process, she does remember wanting to help chondria. Don't think I have any ill-will toward other human beings, or would resort to tricks, or my abilities, to force a hosting. The result of a hostile bonding isn't pleasant. But, that's another story."

I pause, making sure she understands that I would never force her to be like me. In fact, the thought of doing such a thing makes my skin crawl.

She nods, obviously unsure about why this detail is so vital.

"The final thing I have to tell you is that each host gains a number of abilities that are common for all hosts, such as communicating through thoughts instead of out loud. We don't know what it is about chondria that afford us these abilities, but we think they *may have been a much more advanced species than us, or there is speculation that our combined DNA simply creates something more advanced. One of my other abilities is that I can sense when another host is present. There are more, as you have already experienced the first time I touched you. For now, I simply want to tell you about the most important one."*

She sits up hurriedly. "It was your hand on my shoulder that day in the ravine! I knew it. What did you do to me? That stone, you put it in my bag?"

"Please, Marley. There will be time for questions later."

I know she wants to know about our connection, but I have to finish up with the basics first. There's an order to these things. Hell, I train other trackers on how to do this.

She nods reluctantly. "For now."

"Right, so, where was I? Oh yeah, each host gains an ability that is unique based on a natural talent. There are physical and cognitive abilities in my world, and some are a combination of the two. So if you are excellent at finding people or things, you would have an excellent intuition about tracking and a bit of speed to match. If you are physically fit before you become a host, you might be exponentially strong after bonding. A few of the best writers and painters of today are actually hosts. If you are a musician, you would be a virtuoso after. If you are charismatic, you literally have the ability persuade the pants off of anyone. Even people who are scientists or doctors who become hosts gain special talents in their field, and the list goes on and on. Often, it takes time to realize what special ability will be gained, but it is always something unique to that particular host.

"You might have already guessed that my unique ability is that I can track. I can touch anything and sense who or what has touched it before and precisely how long ago. I can pick up scents,

and hear things that are miles away if I focus. That's how my mom and I were able to find hosts for chondria more easily. My mom said it was my destiny to match chondria with hosts. I was the first. In fact, that's my title, First Tracker.

"When Robert, my adopted father, came along, we had the added bonus of gaining access to people who did not want to listen to us. He's a charismatic, and everyone is drawn to him. He's very humble about his ability, even though he could charm or persuade anyone to do anything he wants. Then, shortly after that, my mom found Anna. She was a baby, like me. Her ability revealed itself over time. She has what some would say is the greatest ability among hosts."

I smile and look up at the sky, remembering the first time Anna showed us what she could do.

"Anyway, as far as we can tell, she must have been using more of her brain or a special part that the rest of us rarely use before she became a host. After she bonded with chondria, she started moving objects with her mind. I have always been a little envious."

I glance back down at her face to see her reaction.

She's staring at me, clearly in shock. "Shut...up! You're kidding, right?"

Yep. That's usually the response new recruits have.

"Do you think I could ask her to show me? That would be so cool. Or, is that considered rude?"

"No, actually, Anna loves to show off her ability, privately of course."

"Really? That's so amazing. I mean, I've seen movies about telekinesis, but to see it for real? Wow."

I roll my eyes. I love my sister, but she's always in the limelight. Let's see what her reaction to my mom is. "So now I have told you about my special ability, my dad's, and my sister's. I bet *you're curious about what my mom's is?*" I raise my eyebrows eagerly, a smile playing across my lips.

She shrugs her shoulders, eyes intent on mine, and nods.

"*My mom was a psychic before she became a host.*"

Out loud I say, "Guess what she can do?"

12

Q & A

Marley

A psychic? No, she can't be. I've never bought into that sort of thing, but I also never thought any of the things Will told me were possible either. "So are you saying she can see the future and all that?"

Will's smile gets even bigger. "*My mom has visions that allow her to not only see the future, but also the past and present as well.*"

"So how does that work?"

Will nods and thinks, "*She touches someone or something that belongs to them, and she can see a part of their life unfold. Although her emotions can sometimes get in the way if she is too close to the person. She can't see my future, for example, because she's my mom. But, she's very helpful in tracking down potential hosts.*"

I smile. "That's cool. So then how do you find potential hosts?"

"*Well, as a tracker, my chondria are drawn to potential hosts,*" *so that is the start of the process. My mom's visions help me to track more quickly, as well. Sometimes, she can see me marking a potential host or she gets a vision of a time and place, which serves as a clue. Once I have narrowed it down to a small area, I can detect who the potential host is."*

"Wow. That seems like a lot of work. Do you like doing it?" I ask, genuinely curious.

He seems surprised by my question. *"Huh, no one has ever asked me that before. I guess I do most of the time. It would be nice to have a break every now and then, though."*

"I can't even imagine." My mind is exploding from information overload. I hug my legs and rest my chin on top of my knees and watch the water tumble from stone to stone on its journey downstream. "Can you give me a minute to process? This is a lot to take in."

"Of course, I'm sorry. I know this must be overwhelming for you."

I try to smile, but find it difficult because I'm mulling everything over in my mind. I think about what it might be like to be a host like him. Hmm...wait a minute. Back up. Here I am sitting on a coat, on Tumbling Run Trail, next to my prom date with tiny little aliens in his eyes. This is crazy. What's even crazier is that I like him, despite the story he told me. There's something about him, and it goes beyond mere physical attraction. His story is fascinating, almost unbelievable if I didn't see those little intelligent chondria swirling around in his irises. I wonder what they feel like. That shouldn't be my first question, though, if that is what now is—question time.

I can see in his eyes that he wants to break the silence, but is resisting so that I can get my bearings. Okay, so let me wrap my head around this.

First, Will is a host to intelligent alien life forms, something I have only known through *Star Trek*. Second, they give him special powers, and those powers cannot be found in any normal human being on earth. And third, he's telling me...

"I think I need to ask you a very important question first." I pause, waiting to make sure he's ready.

Will draws his knees up to his chest, resting his arms on top of his knees, mirroring me. "Shoot."

"Why are you telling me all of this? What does all of this have to do with me?" I'm both fascinated and scared to death of the answer, but I'm fairly sure I know.

"I thought you would have realized by this point what your role in all this is." He searches my face for some kind of recognition. When he realizes I need it spelled out, he thinks, "*You are a potential host.*"

That's what I thought. "How do you know that I'm a potential host?" Before he can answer, I can't help but continue, "Also, what did you do to my shoulder, and why did you put that stone in my bag?"

He looks confused about what to answer first.

I shake my head slowly. "Sorry, I know I'm asking a lot all at once. It's just that I have so many questions."

Will takes my hand in his and gently traces my palm with his index finger, sending tiny sparks up and down my arm. "I know. I've given you so much to think about. But listen, I don't want you to worry. I'm not going to force you to do anything, and I'll try to answer your questions to the best of my ability. You don't need to make any kind of decision today. You should take your time. So I'll answer a few questions now, and then we can have some more tomorrow." He takes a deep breath. "So, why you?"

I nod.

"*I selected you because my mom and I honed in on the energy of a potential host the day your class was doing a trail cleanup. My mom had a vision of the trail, at the top of the ravine. As soon as I saw you ahead of me on the trail, well, I knew you were the one. I waited until you found Becca, and Liz took her back down the trail. You were all alone in the ravine. I approached you without you seeing me. I placed my hand on your shoulder to ah...well...I don't want this to sound strange but, to mark you.*" He smiles a little to ease the awkwardness. "*It creates a link between you and me, letting all other trackers know that you have been spoken for. It's only visible for about twenty-four hours, and only hosts and the potential host can see it.*"

"Oh. So that's why my mom couldn't see it," I say, more to myself than to him.

"*Yeah, we have to maintain our secrecy, at least for now. I also gave you a stone that is actually from the original meteorite. We believe the illuminating green streaks are fossilized chondria. Each tracker is given a stone. The live chondria inside the host tracker identify and create a special bond with the fossilized chondria in the stone. I was the first to connect with my stone, so I have a very strong connection to it. So in essence, my stone is linked with my chondria, and the fossilized chondria are connected to all chondria on earth. I gave it to you so that I would know where you are if you need me.*"

Will reaches into his pocket and pulls out the stone. He places it in my hand. "*It's yours, for as long as you want,*" he thinks, a serious expression on his face.

So, I need protection from something. Why would I need

protecting since I've been safe for the last sixteen years of my life? What is different about me now? I roll the stone over in my hand, examining it. The greenish streaks begin to glow. When I look back up at Will, his chondria are swirling around his irises. He closes his eyes and cringes as if in some kind of discomfort.

"Oh, I'm sorry. I wasn't thinking." I put the stone in my pocket.

"*It's all right. Maybe you could contact me only when you really need to?*" he thinks with a pained but teasing tone.

"Yeah, sure." I wonder when that will be...

I look down at his coat, trying to collect my thoughts. "Okay, so let me get this straight. You marked me because I am a potential host for your chondria. You gave me your stone, and I can use it sorta like a pager. And you won't force me to become a host. Have I got it right?"

"*Correct.*"

Next question. "Were you watching me in the ravine when you marked me?"

He smiles, cheeks flaming up, and looks everywhere but at me. "I uh, well, I had to keep an eye on you."

"You saw me without my clothes! Did you at least turn around?" I ask, already knowing the answer. Typical.

He fights a sheepish grin. "Do you want the truth?"

I cross my arms and roll my eyes. "Oh, forget it. I know the truth." Secretly, I wonder if I would have looked too if the roles had been reversed. Yeah, I would have, I think, smiling to myself.

There's one more thing I need to know. "Do you remember in the car when you said we have been spending time together in our dreams? What did you mean by that?"

"*Oh, yeah, I did mention that to you. That's a little compli-cated to explain. My chondria allow me to create and share dreams with others. That's another ability afforded to all hosts. So when you go to sleep, I have the ability to share a dream with you while we sleep. When a host sleeps, he maintains a certain level of consciousness, thanks to chondria. I remember all of my dreams when I wake up in the morning. It takes some time to hone in on the right person with all of the people sleeping. But, ever since I marked you, I have been able to detect you rather quickly. It's a very useful way to pass messages and talk to people without frightening them. They believe it's only a dream. So it's like I'm calling you on the phone late at night, but you're asleep. I can take you to some amazing places if you want. I've traveled extensively with my family searching for potential hosts, so I have many memories. Also, only hosts can initiate and share a dream with another person. In other words, it's not a two-way street between hosts and non-hosts. However, if a person such as yourself should begin dreaming about a certain host on your own, well...*" The corners of his mouth turn up in a smile, and he's blushing again.

"So what are you saying? You know when I have private dreams about you that you didn't share with me?" My cheeks are aflame, turning a shade darker than his, and it's not just from embarrassment. I've had some pretty hot dreams about him. "Are any of my dreams my own? Don't you think that's an invasion of my privacy?" I look away, unable to meet his gaze.

He turns my chin, forcing me to look at him. "No, that is not at all what I'm saying. The only reason I know about those dreams is because we have a special connection since I marked you."

I turn back away, not wanting to face the idea that he knows about my private dreams. It's unnerving!

"No, you don't understand. How can I explain this to you? It's not that I actually know what happens in your dreams or anything. Those dreams are your own. However, since I marked you, I get a strong, let's say, signal from you when you dream about me."

While I'm still a little embarrassed, I begin to grasp his meaning. He doesn't know what I'm dreaming about, just that I am. I relax my shoulders, feeling slightly better. "So, it's kind of like when my mom asks me if my ears were burning because she was talking about me to someone else?"

Will smiles and nods excitedly. "That's it exactly! What a great analogy...except, well, there are no burning ears."

We both laugh. I'm relieved that he isn't able to peek into my private dreams, even though he knows when I have them. On an impulse, I hug him, taking him by surprise. "Thanks for trusting me with all of this. I know I didn't make it easy."

He stiffens, surprised, but recovers quickly, his embrace turning comforting, his cheek resting against my head. "You are so surprising, Marley Hunter." It feels right, and all of my doubts wash away.

I pull back and smile. "I have my moments. Okay then, that about covers what I need to know right now."

"So, is there any chance you still think I'm hot?"

I swat at his chest. "Cool it, Casanova."

He's got the most adorable smile. I can't help but grin back.

I look up at the sky, wondering what planet chondria came from. The world feels vibrant and interesting now that aliens exist for real. Not to mention they are living inside my prom date. I take a few deep breaths, stretching my arms above my head, not wanting to move from this spot, and I can't stop grinning. I feel downright giddy.

"Well, okay then, shall we go meet your parents?"

My smile disappears. I had forgotten about that.

13

A PROPER FIRST DATE

Will

Marley calls her mom as soon as we realize how late we're going to be getting home from Tumbling Run. She looks nervous as she talks on her phone. I should have been more careful of the time. First impressions are everything. We stop back at the school to pick up my car and drive separately to her house. I pull into Marley's driveway behind her around six-thirty. She gets out of her car and waves me to hurry up. As soon as I reach her, she grabs my hand as we hurry inside. She kicks off her sneakers at the door and grabs a pair of black flats. I look down at my shoes wondering if I should take them off, but she says, "Don't worry about it."

She grabs my hand again and pulls me along through her living room. Her house is very charming. It's got that old world feel, like it has a history. Before I can truly assess my surroundings, she's leading me through a kitchen and out a back door to a patio. I can see that Marley is nervous about this meeting. Once I set eyes on her mom, I realize why

Marley's nervous. Her mom doesn't look happy about our tardiness.

"Hi, Mom, sorry we're late. This is Will, my date for the prom," she says warily, stepping out onto the patio. "He's new to the area." She turns to me. "Will, these are my parents, Mr. and Mrs. Jensen."

Jensen?

Marley picks up on my confusion. "Oh, Ray is my stepdad...different last name."

Ah, that's right. I had forgotten. Confidently, I approach Marley's parents as they stand. I can see where Marley's good looks come from. I extend my hand to her mom first. "It's very nice to meet you, Mr. and Mrs. Jensen. I apologize for our tardiness," I say with a polished tone and smile.

Mrs. Jensen's warm smile tells me that it's working. "It's nice to meet you, too, Will. Please call me Susan. I know Marley is very excited to go to the prom." She winks at Marley.

Marley's cheeks turn pink as she scowls. The truth of her mom's declaration sends waves of pleasure through my body. I smile genuinely at Susan and turn and wink at Marley. She's so cute when she's embarrassed. I hope Susan can do it again.

I release Susan's hand and shake Ray's. He has a much firmer grip than his wife. Even though I can't read minds, I can tell he's thinking something along the lines of, 'You'd better treat my daughter right.' I return his firm grip, never breaking eye contact, and nod knowingly. I'll take care of her.

"I guess we should be going?" Marley asks.

She's uncomfortable. She must not bring too many boys home to meet her parents. Good. That's perfectly all right with me.

"We have reservations at...?" She looks at me, anxious for the save.

I pause, watching her squirm a little bit. God, she looks sexy. She's tugging at her long, wavy blonde hair, pulling it to one side, her gray eyes pleading with mine and she bites her bottom lip. Finally, I smile and nod in recognition. "Yeah, we should be going. We have reservations at Tamarind at seven o'clock."

Marley looks surprised at my restaurant choice.

"*Liz told me that you love Tamarind,*" I think to her without moving a muscle.

She jumps, startled. She's going to have to get used to hearing my voice in her head, because I plan to be there often...even when other people are around.

"Marley, what's the matter?" her mom asks.

"Oh, nothing, I got a chill," she explains, brushing it off.

Susan smiles at Ray. "Well, if you wanted to get Marley's attention, you certainly made the right choice. Indian is her favorite."

Marley smiles, a look of relief washing over her.

"I like Indian food too. Must have been a lucky guess." I smile at Marley innocently, as if that were the truth.

Her eyes widen as she shoots me a look of alarm, nodding toward my eyes. They have been so hard to control when I'm around her.

I nod in kind, blinking twice. The single chondria swimming around my left eye is gone before Susan or Ray can notice.

"Well, see ya, Mom. See ya, Ray." She gives her mom a hug and a wave at Ray.

"Yes, very nice to meet you. I hope we'll meet again," I say.

"Be safe, Marley, and *you*," her mom says, pointing at me, pausing to make sure I'm listening, "You take care of my daughter."

We will.

Marley

We arrive at Tamarind a few minutes before seven, and I'm still reeling from the events of the day. How I ended up at my favorite restaurant on a date with Will is beyond me. On the ride over, the cynic in me reared her ugly head. *Why is he really interested in me?* He probably wants to make sure I choose to be a host. More than likely he does this with all potential hosts, and I'm simply another assignment.

Before the host, no pun intended, can seat us, I excuse myself to use the restroom. I've got to see how bad I look since I didn't have any time to get ready after school. I also need a moment alone with my thoughts.

I check myself in the bathroom mirror. I apply some lip gloss and run my fingers through my hair. It's curling into ringlets at the ends. Damn humidity. I glare at myself, thinking I should have listened to Liz when she told me to dress up today. I press my hands on the side of the sink, annoyed. *It's just a date. Get over it.* I adjust my top to hang off my shoulder a bit and turn around to check the back of my jeans. I turn to leave when, oddly, I hear a wicked sing-songish female voice in my head.

"*Not good enough...not even close...*"

I freeze, startled. "Hello? Is someone in here?" I ask, hoping no one answers.

A similar voice from one of the stalls yells, "Obviously. Do you mind?"

Well, excuse me! How rude.

When I emerge from the restroom, Will is still waiting for me at the front of the restaurant. I expected that he would be seated already. He smiles, looking me up and down. "I didn't want to sit without you. Do you have a favorite spot?"

I shrug my shoulders. "Not really."

He nods to the host that we are ready and looks down at my bare shoulder, smiling. Then his arm is around my waist, guiding me forward.

I blush as we are seated at an intimate booth at the back of the restaurant, the menus placed in front of us. "You look great. I think I was so preoccupied with business stuff earlier that I didn't get a chance to tell you." Will picks up his menu and looks it over.

Business? Did he really just say business? "Am I like a job for you?"

He drops his menu and reaches for my hand. "No, Marley, of course not. I only meant that I needed to tell you certain things, and I couldn't enjoy spending time with you until I did." He squeezes my hand. "I'd like to do that now if that's all right with you?"

I feel stupid. I always jump to the wrong conclusion. "Yeah, I'm sorry. I must sound...never mind. Forget I said that, okay?" I try to smile, but it feels more like a cringe.

"Sure. Change of subject. Remember when you told me that I was hot?" He smiles, breaking the tension.

"One freakin' time I said it. You are never going to let that go, are you?" I ask, slapping his arm, playfully.

He laughs. "Easy, girl."

I look down at the menu, pretending to search for something to eat. I don't really need to look since I've pretty much got all the dishes committed to memory. There's always a chef's special, and that's what I get most of the time.

So while I'm pretending to choose, I seize the opportunity to check him out over the top of my menu. His head is tilted, looking down at the menu, and I can't help but think how different he is, even without seeing chondria in his eyes. His skin is unusually tan, not like everyone else's, still pale from the winter months.

Next, my eyes move to his mouth. I wonder what it would be like to kiss him. Are his lips as soft as they look right now? Does he want to kiss me?

Slowly, my eyes trail up to his veiled eyes, cast down. That's his most distinguishing feature—dark eyes, which remind me of the night sky. Except when chondria are in his irises, then it's fireflies at dusk.

His hair is exactly as I remember seeing it the first time in the nurse's office. Dark, messy, and perfect. I wonder if chondria help to make all hosts attractive. He starts to smile, not looking up from the menu.

I smile nervously. He knows I'm watching him.

"So what looks good to you?" I ask with interest to mask my silent admiration.

He looks up from the menu. "Well, everything looks great, but I'm thinking about ordering the special." He grins, taking my hand in his again.

I gasp, feeling tiny sparks of electricity as his hand entwines with mine. "Yeah, that's what I usually do, too. Everything on the menu is great, but it's nice to try something new."

"Then we'll have two specials," he says matter-of-factly.

"Let's ask the waiter what it is first."

"Let's make it a surprise, live dangerously."

I laugh. "You like games, don't you?"

Will's smile widens. "Yeah, I guess I do. Oh, come on..."

"All right. But, if it's goat, you're a dead man."

When our entrees come, I'm pleased to see its chicken tikka masala, one of the most common Indian dishes. We both sigh with relief and then laugh at one another for our obvious concern that we would be eating goat. As I finally begin to relax, I get the odd sensation that I'm being watched. I look up to find the culprit but to no avail. Still, I'm unable to shake the uneasy feeling. I look at Will for some recognition that he feels it too, but he's already scanning the room.

"Do you think someone is watching us?" I ask under my breath.

Will continues to look around the room. I do the same, except I don't have the extra senses that he has. I don't see anyone, but still...

Will covers my hand with his and flashes me a reassuring smile. "I'm sure it was nothing."

Something deep down inside tells me that it wasn't 'nothing.' I'm about to say as much when he begins massaging the soft area between my thumb and index finger.

Oh, that feels nice.

Slowly, as his ministration continues, I forget the creepiness. There's only him and me, and if he keeps touching me like this, I might forget the rest of the world too.

* * *

AFTER DINNER, he asks me if I want to walk in the park across the street from his house. It's a great idea since I don't want our date to end.

The park has a path that loops around jungle gyms, playgrounds, and soccer fields. The path then continues further into a wooded area with a bridge that crosses a stream. Most of the kids that come here hang out on the bridge. Also, it's a pet-friendly park so lots of people walk their dogs here. Tonight isn't as busy as usual, a few couples here and there, and some other kids I know from school.

As we walk along a path close to his house, Will stops me. "Would it be strange for me to ask if we could hold hands? I know this is close to your friend Becca's house, and people from school will probably see us."

Why is he worried about what people will say? I mean I know I'm not the most glamorous girl, but I'm not an embarrassment either! "Do I embarrass you or something? Why don't you want people to see us together?"

"No, no...I meant that if people see us holding hands, they will think we're a couple. I'm cool with that, but are you?" he asks, eyebrows raised.

"Oh. I hadn't thought about that. Look, I'm not very good at this dating thing. I've had a boyfriend, but..." I hesitate, unsure of how much to say about my previous relationship. There were no sparks. Nothing like what I'm feeling now. Better just skip it. I take his hand and interlock our fingers. "I definitely don't mind holding hands with you."

As we continue walking, I'm surprised that he wants to talk about everyday things. All I want to do is ask about his special abilities. There are some things I'm *dying* to know more about. Apparently, his eyesight is beyond anything a regular human can see, and he can pick up scents and noises from miles away. I also learn about the most interesting gift he possesses, his ability to touch things and see in his mind what has touched them in the past. I can't wait to see him in action, so he invites me to watch him track next weekend. He's going to practice for some host competition, and his sister Anna is going to practice her skill as well. I enthusiastically accept.

After that, he wants to talk about me. I start laughing uncontrollably. After the extraordinary talents he told me about, I really don't have anything compelling to tell him. What's worse is he can't understand why I think this is so funny.

With dramatic enthusiasm I say, "So, last night...I washed my hair. I'm trying out a new shampoo. Also, I laid out an outfit to wear for our date, which I never got to put on because you kidnapped me. Let's see, oh yeah, I watched a little TV, and Googled 'do's and don'ts' for a first date." I can barely finish because I'm laughing again.

He finally seems to understand the absurdity of it and laughs with me. "Very funny, Marley. However, maybe some-day, that won't be a joke anymore." He raises a brow, charmingly.

Hmm, I'll have to think about that. "One step at a time, Will," I respond, jokingly, but he's right. I have a very serious decision to make at some point.

He takes me home around nine-thirty, walking me to my front door, nothing uncomfortable about it. I've never been on a date that went so well. I'm not dreading any awkward-ness about saying goodnight.

"I had a really nice time today. I hope you're still okay with everything I told you earlier," Will says.

I meet his eyes. I can't believe how comfortable I am around him, this soon after meeting him. "Here, come with me," I say, pulling him off the porch to the privacy of the side of my house, behind an oak tree out of sight from any windows.

"I can't imagine a more perfect date. I know there were some very strange and extraordinary things you told me, but being with you feels..." I pause, looking up at the cover of green branches and glimpses of night sky filled with stars reminding me of Will's eyes.

I look back down, and his chondria are aglow in his eyes. I gasp. Fireflies at dusk.

"I know I promised you earlier that I would be respectful. But I'm going to kiss you now, and I don't think I can keep that promise."

His lips are on mine before I can respond.

Whoa. I wrap my arms instinctively around his neck, pulling him closer. My eagerness takes him by surprise as I fall back against the cool bark of the tree trunk, bringing him with me. We stand there for a while, bodies intertwined, as the kiss deepens, and I wonder if I'll have the strength to let go.

14

THE HOST WORLD

Will

I don't believe in soul mates, but if I ever needed evidence to the contrary, I just got it in spades. Marley was more than receptive to the kiss. She looked so beautiful looking up at the sky, her lips parted in mid-sentence. My chondria stirred, almost uncontrollably, intensifying my feelings for her a thousand fold. I've kissed girls before, but this? Intense doesn't even cover it.

In the end, I forced myself to back away from her and say good night. I was afraid I might not be able to stop if I kept kissing her. Plus, I really don't want to cloud her judgment. I want it to be *her* choice to become a host, not mine. If that kiss is any indication of her feelings toward me...I don't think I have anything to worry about. How am I going to manage to be around her? It took all my strength to pull away from her, and we only kissed.

I drive home the long way so I can think about everything that transpired today. I can't believe my luck in finding

Marley. My God, if another tracker had found her first...I push the thought from my mind. She took in everything about me, everything I told her, and only faltered once, then recovered nicely. The best part is, I can be myself now, letting my chondria flow freely. She even seems to like looking at my eyes when chondria migrate there.

My chondria are still adjusting to my closeness to her, hurtling through my body when she holds the onyx stone too tightly or when she is upset. They sense their kin permanently frozen within the stone, and their own essence when I marked her shoulder. When I am close to her, they nudge me...*protect*...so strange and uncomfortable even after all this time tracking hosts. I have no idea what the pull is, but my chondria have an intense interest in her, it's... unsettling.

The marking process has a serious impact on both parties. For the tracker, it's an invisible tether to the viable host, always knowing where they are, giving the strength of chondria to them. It's a strange feeling to share my chondria with another. Still, this time, especially for her, I would endure anything. For the potential host, there are tremors and feelings of vertigo for the first few meetings, which Marley clearly felt the effect of. Considering her calmness tonight, though, it seems to be wearing off, a good sign for both of us.

I've been hopeful each time I helped someone bond with chondria, wanting to finally find someone I could connect with. All of the others, even though some were attractive, were not right for me. Marley, on the other hand, is exactly what I've always been looking for. She has the most beautiful smile, and I want nothing more than to see chondria swimming in her gray eyes. The best part is that she loves the outdoors. I could spend every day with her on the trails if I didn't have my responsibilities. I can't help but smile thinking about how she says everything that she's thinking no matter what.

I'll have to be patient with Marley. She'll make her decision. What I need now is a distraction. I plan to practice this weekend for my competition at the Annual Host Gathering. This year, the Gathering will take place on the land of a very wealthy host outside of Flagstaff, Arizona. I'm entered into the hunting competition, having lost to my good friend and fellow tracker, Aiden, last year. It took us two days to finally catch up to that elusive squirrel. I wonder what animal will be selected this year. I haven't had a victory since I was fifteen, and that was only by a small margin. The quarry was a rabbit, and I trapped her a split-second before another competitor. It was a very rewarding win.

I pull into the driveway of my new house only to feel like I just left my true home. My dad will be up reading, as he always is, and Anna will be listening to music in her room. Mom called last night and told Dad she won't be back for a while. She's helping out one of our sister host families. They lost one of their own, and unfortunately, their chondria were not able to be saved. The death of loved ones is tough enough, but dealing with the death of chondria is twice as hard because chondria mourn for their lost kin as well. It's often physically painful. I'm a little lost without her since she's usually by my side when we approach and court potential hosts, but I guess there's a first for everything.

As I walk through the front door, I think, *"Hi, Dad, Hi, Anna, I'm home."*

"*Good evening, son. I left some dessert in the kitchen for you—apple pie,*" my dad thinks from upstairs in his library.

"*Yeah, um, I ate his piece of pie. Sorry,*" Anna thinks without much regret.

"Anna!" Dad yells out loud.

It's just like Anna to do something like this. I don't really mind all that much since I'm still very full from dinner, but my dad likes to cook, so I'm sure he wanted my opinion on his baking skills. "*It's fine. I'm sure it was delicious,*" I think to my dad and Anna.

"*It was good, Dad, both times,*" Anna responds.

"*Anna, you seriously need to work on your manners,*" my dad thinks sternly to both Anna and me.

Then to only me, he asks, "*Will, why don't you come up and tell me about your date?*"

I take my time walking up the steps and down the hall to my dad's library. My dad loves to read and spends his time this way in the evenings. His library is filled with hundreds of books about everything under the sun: biographies, botany, cooking, science, history, self-help, psychology, sociology, philosophy, politics, and even some fiction. He prefers non-fiction, but every now and then I see a shelf with a few murder mystery titles. When I open the door, he's sitting in one of the two high-backed chairs in front of a large bay window that overlooks the backyard.

I slump down in the chair next to him, yawning. "Well, what do you want to know?"

My dad shakes his head in disapproval but smiles. "All right, Will, a few questions. How did Marley react to our secret?"

"Well, at first she freaked out, but then she came around."

Before he can ask anything else, I eagerly continue, "There's something about her, too. She's so different from the other potential hosts I've marked. It's like I have this special connection with her or something."

He studies me with a mixture of surprise and approval. "I've never heard you speak about someone like this before. What's so different about her?"

I smile. Where do I begin? We talk for a while about all the things I like about Marley. I confide that I want more than anything for her to become a host. He's very happy that I found someone I like spending time with, but slightly concerned about my intensity. His advice is to be patient and understand that it's her choice to become a host, not mine. I can't help but be a little nervous because of what happened the last time I found a potential host.

"Dad, what do you think the Council is going to do about the problem down in Texas?"

The World Council of Hosts meets at the Annual Host Gathering to discuss issues the hosts and chondria face and also plan for the future, but they sometimes convene throughout the year if there are pressing matters. Mom was the chairperson of the Council for quite a few years, but stepped down when I was fourteen to allow someone else a chance to lead.

"Well, your mother said they are waiting for the Gathering to discuss it since there has only been one incident in the past six months. *You* feel the urgency because it happened to you."

He's right, of course. We were in Austin, trying to recruit a very special potential host. The day before I was going to mark him, someone else abducted him. When I approached his house, I could sense the other host, and when I touched the window by his bedroom, I knew exactly which host had taken him. Malcolm Durst.

I'm sure he followed us to Austin and correctly identified the potential host. That poor boy is no doubt a razer, serving Malcolm and his family.

Razer is the term used for a host who has been forced to bond with chondria and lost his or her ability to think for themselves. The only people who can get through to a razer are those who share the same chondria. The Dursts are careless and cruel, and this isn't the first time they've done something like this. I still wonder what made my mother bond Malcolm to begin with. His special gift is strength, but he has a mean streak a mile long. How did my mother not see that?

"I know, Dad, but I wish we had a cure for razers. I feel completely responsible for that boy, and we don't even know where he is. I waited too long," I say, sad and frustrated. Medical hosts are experimenting with some success. Occasionally, a razer starts to come out of their strange hazy trance, but a relapse always occurs. I hope that someday we have a permanent solution.

"I know it's terrible to think about. But, you know we will find an answer."

I stand. As I open my mouth to say good night, he interrupts me, "Will, I know you're tired, but I'm afraid you have some business to attend to now."

"Oh no. Now what?" I sit back down in the chair.

My dad sighs. "Your latest tracker is having problems again with his abilities. I don't know if he can be helped, but if anyone can, it would be you. I know it's the last thing you want to deal with, but Aiden is, of course, nowhere to be found at the moment. It won't take you more than an hour or so. Will you meet with him?"

Dustin Kelly. I groan and consider that it may be a long night. I bonded Dustin four months ago and turned him over to Aiden to train once we realized his gift was tracking. Dustin has proved to be a trial. He clearly has the gift to track, but he has little to no faith in those abilities. Most new trackers take about two to three months to train. Dustin is going on four months. "I guess," I say with absolutely no enthusiasm.

"I'm sorry, son. Sometimes these things take time." He's trying to look on the bright side as usual.

I roll my eyes. "Yeah, yeah. I better get going if I'm going to get any real sleep tonight." And I'm out the door on my way to my room.

My last thought before I drift off is that I wish I could dream about Marley instead...

"WILL, THANK GOD YOU'RE HERE!" Dustin shouts emphatically, shaking my hand. Then, as if noticing his surroundings for the first time, he asks, "Where exactly are we?"

"Hi, Dustin. We are in my dream at the Annual Host Gathering from two years ago," I say, indifferently, looking around at the jungle surrounding us. "This Gathering was situated on private land in the Yucatán peninsula in Mexico. You will be able to explore all aspects of this area that any host experienced. Your chondria will access other chondrias' memories. So don't worry about not having attended."

"A real Host Gathering? Are you freakin' serious? Oh...

my...God! This is awesome!" Dustin is barely listening to my instructions, his floppy blond hair flying about as he dances around excitedly. No wonder he's having issues.

I glare at him, knowing I need to get this overt giddiness under control. "Okay, calm down, Dustin. You're eighteen years old, and you're acting like a little kid. The only reason you're here is so we can work on your skills. Follow my lead and keep your mouth shut unless I ask you a question. Is that clear?"

Dustin stops his silly antics. "Yes, of course. I'm sorry, it's just that I haven't been able to attend a Gathering yet."

"Okay, I know," I say dismissively. "Now, what have you been having problems with?"

"Problems with?" he replies, seeming to not understand what I'm asking.

I glare back at him with my hands on my hips.

A light seems to turn on in his head. "Oh, yeah, I can't get the whole sensing, touching thing down. I thought I had it, but now I can't visualize anything."

"I see," I reply, wondering if this night will ever end. Only some trackers have this ability. Unfortunately for me right now, this includes Dustin. "Come with me."

Dustin follows me over to a large hay bale standing on its end. I touch it first and see my sister, Anna, the reigning champion of no-touch archery aiming at a target in the distance. I love watching her compete. In my mind, I can see her aiming her arrow so perfectly with only her mind, and at such a long distance. She hits the target, dead center. Amazing! Her skill makes me wonder if there's a relationship between the amount of brain use and potential host compatibility, which is why we are gaining numbers in the telekinesis area.

I open my mouth to tell Dustin it's his turn, when I'm interrupted by none other than Anna, herself. "It's all a matter of practice."

"Anna, what are you doing here?" I ask, annoyed. This evening is not turning out at all like I planned.

"I'm bored, and since I'm already here... Why don't I help you?"

"This is perfect! We're going to have so much fun!" Dustin hoots excitedly.

I mumble grumpily, "No, Anna. I'm training Dustin."

Anna makes her best pouty face. "I'll be on my best behavior. I promise...please...please...."

I roll my eyes. "Fine, let's walk. But if you get annoying, you're out of here."

Anna squeals enthusiastically as she looks around. "Will, your memories of this Gathering are so vivid!"

We walk past the main stage, part of the Mayan ruins. This is where the opening speech was given. It reminds me that our dad is scheduled to give that speech at this year's Gathering.

Anna grabs my sleeve and points to an area of the jungle that has underbrush removed. Perfect. I walk up to a table that was left behind and place my hand on it. At the same time, I motion for Dustin to do the same.

"Feel everything at once. Listen to your chondria, Dustin. They will guide you." I close my eyes. Now barren, this table housed cakes, barbecue, and new varieties of vegetables and fruit from cooking competitions. The competitors brought their own gas-fueled equipment and tents to maintain their secret recipes and methods. We have some truly gifted horticulturalists and chefs.

I open my eyes. "What do you see?"

"Oh wow! I see limes with watermelon inside, peas with tiny cherry tomatoes hidden in their pods, a coconut with pineapple inside, a chocolate mint plant, a giant mushroom in the shape of a pepper, and a kiwi fruit that peels like a banana." He opens his eyes, a gigantic smile plastered on his face. "I'm so hungry now!"

"That's good. Now, can you see any hosts who touched the table?"

Dustin closes his eyes again, seeming to concentrate. After a moment, he opens his eyes, shaking his head. "Nothing."

"Don't worry, you'll get the hang of it," Anna reassures him. "I can tell you that I was here, and I ate too much cake and an ear of peas. The cake was delicious, but gave me a stomachache; the peas-on-the-cob looked cool, but was so-so on taste."

I glare at Anna. "*I thought you were going to be quiet?*"

"*Jeez, soooorrrryyyy!*"

Just then Dustin takes off running to another cleared area. "Dustin! Wait up!" I yell, as Anna and I follow him.

He stops abruptly. "There was a lion here!"

Good. He's sensing the animal whisperer show that was here. One of the most popular events at the Gathering showcases hosts who speak to animals, called creature hosts. The show is similar to a human circus, but the animals are very exotic and considered untamed to humans.

I reach him and sense the same as he does. "Good job, Dustin. Yes, this was the animal whisperer show."

"Say, tell me about a favorite act?" Dustin asks, hopeful.

I look over at Anna with my eyebrows raised, indicating she should answer him as it is one of her favorite shows at the Gathering.

"Well, at the Gathering in France I saw a creature host walking next to a lion with a child on its back. It was an incredible experience, and the child and lion were great. I swear the lion smiled at the crowd."

"Wow, I can't wait to go to my first Gathering!" Dustin's excitement is palpable.

As we walk around the back of the stage area, I notice an old playing card barely visible under some brush. I pick up the card, the king of hearts. "Hey, Anna, do you remember how I sent you to look for Aiden to play a game of Host Spades here?"

Anna blushes. "Yes, I remember. How could I ever forget? Aiden's mouth was stuck to some new tracker. Aiden couldn't remember her name."

"That was the last time you ever went to go find Aiden for me," I say, laughing.

"There are card games too?" Dustin asks, intrigued again. His big brown eyes widen as his enthusiasm about the Gathering continues. "Will, you and I have to partner up for the next Gathering!"

Host card games require bantering both aloud and in thought. Each player challenges their opponents through thoughts while their facial expression may display a different story. Since I'm considered to be among the best at bluffing, especially when I partner with Aiden, I'm not really looking for a new partner. "I'm not so sure about that, Dustin. Aiden and I usually partner up for cards." I can't imagine Dustin bluffing. He seems to wear his emotions on his sleeve.

We continue to move around the grounds, ending up back at center stage.

"I wish I could sing. I have the worst voice. Do you remember the opera singer? She was awesome," Anna says.

"Dustin, go get on stage and tell me what you feel." I push him forward.

Dustin climbs the steps and walks to the center of the stage, closing his eyes. "I can hear the music that was played here! I hear classical, folk, and rock."

"That's good. Now can you see the actual performers?"

Dustin seems to concentrate even harder, but he opens his eyes, shaking his head. I climb the steps and stand next to him to be sure. I close my eyes and see the opera singer competing against the rapper in the final competition. Afterward, they performed a duet together after the opera singer won. It makes me wonder if Marley will like the music at the Gatherings. It's definitely a highlight for many of the female hosts.

"Okay, Dustin. I think what's happening is that you are not connecting with your chondria in the right way. It's almost like you have to let them take over and show you the images. Let's try this. Where is your onyx stone?"

Dustin reaches into his pocket and pulls out his piece of meteorite. "Okay, now what?"

"Give it to me."

He hands it over, and I throw it as far into the jungle as I can.

His chondria swirl in his irises. "What did you do that for?"

The connection between his chondria and the stone will create an intense pull. "Now, go find it."

Dustin takes off after his stone.

Anna smiles at me. *"You are so mean, Will."*

"What? He has to learn."

A few minutes later, I hear Dustin yelling from a distance. "I found it! Will, you have to come here. I found something else too!"

Anna and I head over to him. Dustin has his hand on a tree. He looks up. "You fixed me, Will. I can see the people who met here in this very spot."

"I knew you had it in you. You need to have faith in your abilities. So what's up? I'm betting Aiden with a girl." That would be about right, considering we're in a dense, secluded area of the jungle.

Dustin's face turns grim. "No, Will. Malcolm Durst was here, and he was meeting with a non-host."

I stride over to where Dustin is standing, put my hand on the tree, and close my eyes. He's right. Malcolm Durst *was* here, and he was meeting with someone. I've never seen the man before, but based on the fact that he was wearing his sidearm in the same place that Agent Rushmore wears his, it seems obvious who he works for. He's FBI. Now, why would an FBI agent help Malcolm Durst?

"Good work, Dustin." I look back at Anna and nod. Now I have confirmation of Malcolm's contact in the FBI, but still no real proof or motive.

15

THE MALL

Marley

I wake to sunlight streaming through one of my fan windows, warming my face. As soon as my eyes focus, my alarm goes off. I reach for it quickly, shutting it off. If I didn't set my alarm on the weekends, I don't think I would ever get up. Lying back down, the first thing that enters my mind is the last thing I had thought about before I fell asleep last night. My date with Will. It's real. I'm dating a host for aliens.

Then my mind travels to the most important aspect of the night—the kiss. I smile and cover my face with the covers, trying not to squeal loudly. I wonder if it felt as awesome for him as it did for me.

I hear my mom and Ray downstairs, busy in the kitchen, getting their morning coffee, and I peek out from my covers. I stretch my legs, wanting to stay in bed and think about Will. Yesterday still feels like a dream. But it's not. It's all very, very real.

I'm a potential host.

I purse my lips and wonder what chondria feel like. Do they hang out in certain places or do they do things in there? What could be my special talent? I like to do lots of things, but I'm not what someone would call talented, let alone *gifted*. I could be a tracker like Will, but something about it doesn't seem right. I like the outdoors and all, but I hate hunting, which is pretty much what tracking is without the killing. I wonder if Will has any thoughts about what my ability would be.

I run through everything Will told me yesterday at Tumbling Run. I don't want to forget even the smallest detail. It's not every day a boy talks about himself like this, let alone a boy with aliens in his eyes. Every potential host becomes a part of the family of the host that bonds them, and chondria have divided up into families across the world. A new host is biologically loyal to his or her own family because they share the same chondria. I wonder how often he meets up with other host families. And, if I become a host, will I be allowed to stay with my parents? I absolutely need to know this before I make any decision.

There's something else bugging me too. Will told me that each potential host has a choice, and no one is ever forced into it. There has to be more to it than that; didn't he say something about 'another story'?

I groan, too much thinking. I'm hungry, and it's time to get up.

I have plans with Liz and Becca today. We're going to have lunch and hit the mall. I still need shoes to match my dress for prom. After a run, a long shower, and eggs on toast, I head out the door to Liz's waiting car. She drives a new red Volkswagen Jetta, which was a birthday present from her parents. Her parents are well off, but it wasn't about getting her an extravagant gift, it was about getting her a reliable necessity. Liz is smiling like crazy. She always smiles, which is part of the reason I love her, but today she's positively beaming, and I know why. She loves the mall.

I slide into the passenger seat and reach for the seatbelt. "Hey, Liz, what's up?"

Liz is wearing a plaid dress with a hot pink sweater. There is a chill in the air this morning, but it's supposed to warm up by afternoon. She has her hair combed perfectly in a pony-tail, and her makeup and jewelry are flawless right down to the matching pink lipstick and earrings. How she manages to look so put together all the time, I'll never know. I'm wearing denim capris, a t-shirt, and Chapstick. My hair is also in a ponytail, but I used my fingers to put it up. Hey, it's Saturday, and it's the Pine Grove Mall.

"Not much," she says, still smiling. "How about you, Miss I-went-on-a-date-last-night-with-a-gorgeous guy?" She giggles and looks at me expectantly.

To be honest, I am rather happy. I grin, remembering the evening with Will. "I'm good. We had a really nice time at *Tamarind*." I accentuate the last part, so she knows that I'm aware of her suggestion to Will. I look ahead at the road, and then back at Liz, eyebrows raised. "Should we go? Where's Becca?"

Liz laughs. "Okay, okay, nice time, happy, want to go look at shoes...got it. I picked you up first because Becca is running late. We're on our way to pick her up now."

Becca lives near Liz, so we have to drive back over toward her neighborhood, which also happens to be where Will lives. I wonder if I'll catch a glimpse of him. I glance down at my clothes. If I had known, I would have tried a little more in getting ready.

I smile at the picture of a Chihuahua taped to Liz's dash. She volunteers at the local animal shelter with Mrs. O'Leary as often as she can get hours. She loves animals and spends a lot of time trying to find homes for the strays. She's almost as nice to people as she is to animals. I envy her conviction. I glance over at her. She's singing loudly along with Katy Perry's "Firework." She has a decent singing voice, but she's so dramatic. She winks at me and blows me a kiss. She's too funny.

We pick up Becca, who looks like I do. She's not a morning person at all. Unfortunately for me, there's no Will Reed in sight, so we head to the mall. Our plan is to shop first and then grab lunch, a salad for me. I find some purple strappy heels at the first shoe store.

Liz applauds as I try them on. "They are meant for you, girl."

They have little sparkles all over the straps and will complement my dress perfectly. "Oh!" I shriek, stumbling, adjusting to walking in the heels. I'm much more of a sneaker and boots kind of girl. I hope I don't break an ankle in these things.

"You'll get used to it," Liz says.

Liz's dress and shoes had been found a while ago, since Mike asked her last fall. He wanted to make sure he snagged her early. Becca is still looking for shoes for her dress. We go to two more stores before she finally finds a perfect, sophisticated pair of open-toed pumps.

"Wow, these are it! I don't care how much they are." Becca

smiles wide, admiring her new find. Must be nice. Mine were on the clearance rack.

As Becca takes off her new shoes, I notice a man outside the store watching us. He's average height, wearing a black suit and tie, a pair of sunglasses, and very short brown hair. Is this new mall security? Boy, shoplifting must be high. Why is he watching us? Do we look like the type to steal? I try to make him look away by staring back. After a few seconds, he does, but before I can point him out to Liz and Becca, he's gone.

Why would someone be watching three teenage girls? Ca-Reepy...

After lunch, Liz and Becca drop me back at my house. I promise to text them later and head out back to catch some rays. I want some time to myself, and a little sunny glow for the prom won't hurt. I change into a tank top and shorts, grabbing some suntan lotion. My mom is outside in the garden planting some spring onions. I wave, heading to the chaise lounge. After getting the right SPF on my exposed areas, I lean back, closing my eyes. Prom is two weeks away, and I can barely wait.

16

AGENT JEFFREY RUSHMORE

Marley

When a man with a navy blue suit and striped tie comes knocking on my front door the next Friday after school, I realize it isn't the first time I've seen him. I open the door, leery. He takes off his familiar aviator-style sunglasses as our eyes meet.

"Hello, Miss. I'm Jeffrey Rushmore, an agent with the Federal Bureau of Investigation," he states simply, flashing a badge. "Might I have a word with you?"

"Um, okay, my parents aren't home right now. Do you want to leave a message for them?" I respond, partially closing the door to avoid what I know is coming.

The man looks confused, and then, when my meaning registers, he nods in understanding. "No, no, I'm not here to talk to your parents, Marley. I'm here to speak with you," he says, smiling. "You are Marley Hunter, correct?"

"Yes," I say, not liking where this is going.

"Look, I'll understand if you don't want to invite me in until your parents get home, but it is imperative that I speak to you as soon as possible."

Okay, this is weird. "Can you tell me what this is regarding?"

"Of course. I recently obtained information that you have made the acquaintance of one William Reed? Is this correct?"

"Um, yeah, I met him, he goes to my school now," I say as calmly as I can. Where's he going with this?

He smiles. "Not to worry, Miss Hunter. Mr. Reed and I know each other fairly well. I am, how shall I put this, his liaison to my particular department at the Bureau."

Well, that's somewhat reassuring, but I don't entirely trust him. I wish Will could be here with me...wait a minute... I smile, finding a newfound confidence. "I'm sorry, how rude, of course you can come in." I show him to the living room, offering him a seat. "Can I get you something to drink? A soda or water?" I ask, hoping he says yes.

He meets my eyes, considering my offer. "Why, yes, if it's not too much trouble, I would love a glass of water."

Yes! I go into the kitchen to get his water and also to rummage through my backpack sitting on the counter. I yell from the kitchen, "I'll just be a minute." I find what I'm looking for and press it firmly into my palm. I picture Will in my head and squeeze it tightly. Okay, I hope this does the trick. I put it back in my backpack and grab the glass of water.

After handing Agent Rushmore the glass, I sit down on the couch across from him, wondering if my attempt to contact Will worked.

Agent Rushmore takes a few sips of water and places it on a coaster on the coffee table.

"So what's this about?"

"Miss Hunter, I believe you are in danger, and that danger has everything to do with your relationship with William Reed."

I look down at my hands. This is not what I expected him to say. I'm in danger because of Will? Who is after me? Does he mean Will would hurt me? I open my mouth to ask these very questions when the doorbell rings. Dang it! Why did I rub the stone? I should have been worrying about myself, not Will!

Agent Rushmore looks toward the door, reaching inside his coat. "Were you expecting someone?"

Whoa! Hold on! This is getting a little crazy. There's an FBI agent sitting in my living room reaching in his jacket for what I assume is a gun, and I'm pretty sure my alien prom date is at the front door. Could this get any stranger? Jeez.

"Actually, yes, I'm expecting Will this afternoon," I say uneasily. "Is that a problem? You said that you two knew each other."

Agent Rushmore removes his hand from his jacket without a gun and appears relieved. "Yes, that's right. I wanted to be sure you were expecting company."

I rise to answer the door. Will is going to have a lot of explaining to do when this is all said and done. When I open the door, Will is standing there, his eyes lit up like a Christmas tree with only green lights. Not blinking, I put up my hand to warn him. "Hey, Will, thanks for coming over. You look all bright-eyed today. I have a guest right now. I think you know him, an Agent Rushmore?"

Will nods in understanding. "*Understood, I'll handle this,*" he thinks in his unique way. Then aloud, "Really? That's interesting. Would you mind if I come in to say hello?"

When I see that his eyes have returned to their normal black color without the little twinkling lights, I respond, "Sure, come on in," and move away from the door.

Agent Rushmore stands and meets Will halfway across the living room. They stare at each other, not saying anything. Then Agent Rushmore glances in my direction and Will nods. Maybe this wasn't such a good idea. They both look so stern, angry almost.

Finally, Agent Rushmore speaks. "I don't care, Will. Damn it, you can't keep doing this. There are dangers involved. Miss Hunter could get hurt. We need to put our heads together and take care of this Austin business once and for all. You know we can't do it on our own. We need you and your family's help."

Agent Rushmore looks visibly frustrated. Will backs away and sits down on the couch and puts his head in his hands. I can tell this exchange, both the one I can hear and the one I can't, isn't going as planned. I'm starting to think there is some truth to what the agent said about my life being in danger.

Will finally looks up. "I understand what you're saying, Jeff, but now is clearly not the time and not in front of Marley," he says, exasperated. "Why did you come here anyway? To scare her? Do you really think this helps anything?"

"No, Will, I came here because I'm worried, and you are not keeping me in the loop this time around. I don't appreciate it, and I will certainly not tolerate it. My job is to protect your life and hers. If you don't keep in contact with me, I have a very difficult time doing that." He looks out the living room window, perhaps contemplating what to say next. While he's doing said contemplating, I'm boiling over.

"Wait one minute, both of you," I start, my voice slow and sharp. I point to Agent Rushmore, feeling anger building. "You have a lot of nerve coming into my house and telling me that I'm in danger, and to think my parents could have been here for that. I also don't appreciate being stalked. You've been watching me for a while now, haven't you? Don't try to deny it. I know it was you watching me with my friends on Saturday at the mall. We were trying on shoes, for God's sakes, and you...you were watching us. That's downright creepy. What are you, like fifty?" Agent Rushmore's cheeks turn a shade of red, as they should.

Then I turn to Will. "And you," I say vehemently, putting my hands on my hips. "You better start explaining right now why my relationship with you has brought an FBI agent into my house. I'm in high school, and going to my prom in a week, with you, no less." I take a deep breath and look from one to the other. "So here it is...you BOTH need to start talking about what is going on here, or I am going to kick both of you out on your asses!" As I finish my rant, my mom walks into the living room.

"Marley! What's going on here?" she asks, looking at me, Will, and Agent Rushmore.

Oh crap. I've seen that look before. She's super annoyed. "Hey, Mom, I can explain—"

Agent Rushmore interrupts me. "No, please let me."

"Hold on a minute, whoever you are. And you better have

some I.D., by the way," my mom says, cutting him off. She turns to Will. "Will, time for you to go home."

"I'm sorry, Mrs. Jensen. I—"

"Save it, Will. Now get going."

Will frowns and thinks to me, "*I'm sorry.*" Then he's out the door.

My mom turns her glare to me. "Marley, go up to your room. I didn't raise you to talk that way to anyone, especially an adult."

I open my mouth to say something but think better of it. I don't want to piss her off anymore. As soon as my feet hit the second floor, my mom says, "All right, now let's see some I.D."

I CHANGE and get into bed. I'm tired and really need to block out the afternoon.

Mom came up to talk to me after Agent Rushmore left. As it turns out, he explained that there was some kind of misunderstanding and that Will's family is helping him in a classified ongoing investigation. I wonder how my mom perceives the 'misunderstanding.' He also insisted that he has not been watching me. He claims that the only time he saw me was at the mall.

I roll over on my side and close my eyes, feeling tired. But real sleep isn't in the cards. Will wants to dream. As soon as I see him, he apologizes again for everything that happened. He reassures me that I'm safe. I can't stay angry with him, and I don't want to waste the dream rehashing this afternoon's events. He takes my hand, and I close my eyes. A rush of air envelopes me as he whisks me to our favorite place. I open my eyes to Tumbling Run. He pulls me down onto a blanket next to the trickling waterfall trail, looking up at the night stars.

"Can I ask you something kind of strange?" I ask.

"Sure," he says, his eyes still on the night sky.

"What do they feel like? Your chondria?"

He smiles up at the stars. "I've been waiting for you to ask me that."

I move closer to him, and he lifts his arm so I can lay my head on his chest.

"Well, for the most part, I don't feel them at all. But when I'm tracking, with a potential host, or another host is nearby, I can sense them moving around in here." He takes my hand and places it on his chest. "And as you know, here." He moves my fingertips to his temple, next to his eye.

"Does it hurt?"

"Not really, it feels...strange. Some older female hosts have said it reminds them of movement of a baby during pregnancy, just more frantic. I've obviously never experienced anything like that so I wouldn't know."

"How do they tell you stuff? Can you hear them?"

"You're just full of questions, aren't you?" He brushes my hair off my forehead. "Well, I don't really 'hear' them. It's more like images and feelings they put in my mind."

I lift my head up to meet his eyes. "So they don't actually talk to you?"

"Not yet, but we're hopeful. We have doctors working on the problem. It's some kind of compatibility issue between chondria and hosts, something about our DNA not having an extra strand necessary to communicate on their level. The current research, which is something my mom follows pretty closely, indicates that there are some rare human beings who have the extra strand in their DNA that could allow them to communicate through language with chondria, but it's really only a theory right now."

I prop up on my elbows. "Why is it just a theory?"

"Well, because we haven't found a human who has the special marker on their DNA *and* is compatible with chondria."

"That would be a problem. So then, do they show you images? Like what?"

Will pulls me back down next to him, my head on his shoulder. "The first time I ever saw you, my chondria showed me an image of you in my arms at Tumbling Run. They've never felt that way about any other potential host before." He looks down at me. "Weird, huh?"

I nuzzle closer to him. "Not at all. It's kind of romantic actually."

He kisses my hair and looks back up at the sky. "I often wonder where chondria came from. The universe is huge. Maybe once we can truly understand them, we'll know their purpose."

Studying the stars, I consider how strange it is that most humans don't believe in aliens considering the size of the universe. Of course, since I know the truth now, it seems obvious. I smile. "Yeah, it seems to go on forever, and all the stars are so beautiful."

"Like you," he says, his eyes smoldering as he leans toward me.

Just as we are about to kiss, an invisible force surrounds

me, suffocating me, dragging me up through the air away from Will.

"Will, help me! What's happening?" But, I can no longer see him. The next thing I know, I'm reaching for my phone on my nightstand.

17

PRACTICE MAKES PERFECT

Will

I sit up in bed with a start. I sensed another host attempting to join our dream as she was pulled out. I grab my phone. Thankfully she's already texted me. She's okay. Even though I would feel better driving over to her house to see her in person, I know I'll see her soon enough in the morning. I'll notify Jeff Rushmore about the incident, but there isn't much he will be able to do.

I've been trying to keep this one quiet for obvious reasons. I will not lose Marley to Malcolm, and I still don't know the connection between Malcolm and his contact at the bureau. Plus, Jeff might even be friends with Malcolm's contact. Sometimes it's a pain being watched by agents all the time, but it's the price we have to pay for letting the government in on our secret society.

There are FBI agents stationed throughout the U.S. keeping tabs on all of our host families. It's in the government's best interest to keep chondria safe, as long as there is no danger to humans or misuse. However, the rest of the world's governments are not as strict. There are some countries that take the surveillance of hosts seriously, such as England, Japan, and Australia. But, there are also plenty of other countries where the government is unaware of hosts or look the other way. It's in those countries that most razers are created.

Still, Agent Rushmore shouldn't have gone to Marley's house today. I don't mind that he's keeping an eye on her, as it can't hurt, but I can't have him scaring her. Jeff and I patched things up after we left Marley's and my dad helped to smooth things over. I agreed to call in more often, and he agreed to keep a watch, out of sight, on Marley.

I wonder what Marley's mom is thinking about the whole incident. She was very unhappy when she walked into her living room to find a strange man with her daughter unsupervised. In the end, she seemed to accept the excuse Jeff gave her, but I could tell she was skeptical. I hope Marley isn't in too much trouble, seeing as this is entirely my fault. Before I left her house, she assured me that she would still be able to go with me tomorrow to watch me practice for the Gathering, and I hope it's still true. Maybe she'll feel better knowing she wasn't the only one who got in trouble; my dad reamed me out when I got home too.

My mind drifts back to the new development. Who was trying to join our dream? The only thing I know for sure is that it wasn't Malcolm. So who?

I climb out of bed. "*Anna, you awake?*"

"*I am now,*" she thinks grumpily after a few minutes.

I grab a t-shirt and slip it over my head and head to her room. "Come in," she says before I can even knock.

Anna is sitting up in bed, yawning and stretching. "I felt someone else enter a dream I was having with Marley. It wasn't you, was it? Have you felt any other hosts that shouldn't be here?"

"Hmm...no, not me. I haven't sensed anyone, but that doesn't mean it isn't so. You're much better at that than I am. Although, your mind has turned into mush ever since you met Marley. I think we should send a message to Mom. She should come back."

"She has enough on her plate. You and I can handle this, and I'll tell Jeff to be on the lookout."

Anna shrugs her shoulders. "Okay, if you say so." She leans back on her pillows and yawns again. "Now if you don't mind, I would like to go back to sleep so we can practice tomorrow. Are you bringing Marley with you?"

"Yeah, I can't wait to show her my skills." I flex my biceps. Anna rolls her eyes.

"Okay, brother. Well, you better get some sleep too and stop spending so much time dreaming with Marley. That girl will be exhausted."

"*Night, Anna*," I think and close her door behind me.

I WAKE up the next morning with a smile. I'll be spending the day doing my favorite thing with my favorite person. I jump out of bed and am in and out of the shower in less than ten minutes. By the time I hit the bottom step, I think, "*Anna! Time to get up! I want to get started!*"

From the kitchen, Anna replies, "I already ate, Will. I've been waiting for you."

Damn, she's fast. I grab a quick bowl of oatmeal, and we're in the car on our way to pick up Marley. She's waiting outside for us when we pull up, wearing jeans, a lightweight t-shirt, a sweatshirt tied around her waist, boots, and a big smile. I get out of the car to meet her on the walkway.

I smile uncontrollably. "Hi, Marley, are you ready to go?"

"Yeah, and I can clearly see from your enthusiasm that you're ready to go, too." She looks over my shoulder. "Hi, Anna."

"Hi, Marley, sorry we're late. Will took forever getting ready," Anna responds, giggling.

"Anna, knock it off, you're embarrassing me." We may be different from other humans, but she certainly makes me feel like we have a very ordinary sibling relationship. It's probably because we're so close in age.

"Okay, I get it, so don't have a temper tantrum," Anna thinks back sardonically.

I turn my attention back to Marley. "Okay, we'd better get going."

It's a beautiful day in the Appalachians; the sun is shining, and a light breeze is moving through the trees. I inhale, smelling pine and musty earth. The trickling of water tells me there's a stream nearby. We are deep in the woods, in a small clearing of grass surrounded by evergreen and birch trees. I'm thankful for my boots since the grass is wet, and there's always the chance a snake could be sunning in the taller grass. I can't wait to begin tracking. I wonder what she will think about my ability. Clearly, Anna's special ability is overtly cool, my skill subtler. I hope Anna selects something small and challenging for me.

Anna moves around the clearing, searching for the right

specimen. I explain to Marley that Anna is looking for an animal for me to track. As luck would have it, there's a chipmunk scurrying past a nearby tree. No sooner than I spot it, Anna picks it up using her abilities, setting it down in front of me.

"Will this do for today, Will? He sure is cute," Anna says, smiling.

"Yes, and it's she, not he," I say, glancing at Marley to see her reaction.

She appears shocked, but then a smile spreads across her lips. "Wow, I mean...really, wow! Anna, your ability is amazing. What happens next?"

I scowl, feeling hurt that she only seemed to notice Anna, not me. Oh well.

I explain to Marley how Anna will tie a small ribbon to the chipmunk and place it somewhere in the forest. Then I'll use my senses to track it. She seems to understand, but still unimpressed with my ability. Figures. I watch Anna and Marley leave the clearing to head back to the car. Anna will release the chipmunk down the road, and let me know when I can begin tracking. I look at my watch and set it for two hours, thinking it shouldn't take much longer than that once she gives me the signal.

While I wait, my mind wanders to whether or not Marley is seriously considering a host life. She seems to like Anna; they would probably even be good friends. She'll meet Dad later today, but I have no idea when she'll finally meet Mom. I realize that Marley and I are as similar as we are different. Even though she likes the outdoors as I do, she likes to do some things I have absolutely no interest in. She was a cheerleader, played the clarinet for a few years, and likes cooking.

How odd. Most potential hosts have a passion for something or at the very least, an expertise, be it a strong career, special interest, or hobby. Marley's passion for the outdoors made me think she would be a tracker at first. But, she has a distaste for hunting. No, she won't be a tracker. I guess I'll have to wait and see.

My thoughts are interrupted by the sense that another host is in the vicinity. I turn and see my buddy and fellow tracker, Aiden McConnell. Aiden became a host at age eleven, and even though he had been living abroad for a few years, he moved back to his hometown of Ayr in Scotland. He's been living there for the past six months. It's curious that he's here in the States. He's wearing his favorite tracking gear —a pair of beat-up sweatshorts, a pair of sneakers, and a super tight t-shirt exposing all of his upper body strength. I roll my eyes. He's a favorite among lady hosts with his sandy blond hair, freckles, and extra bright blue eyes.

His chondria mutated to blue instead of the original green. Chondria can physically mutate depending on the DNA of the host. Aiden and his family all have blue chondria. As far as we know, there have been only two major mutations of chondria. The first occurred with Malcolm Durst, and then the hosts he bonded. Their chondria are purple. The second mutation occurred later with Aiden's adopted host father. His chondria turned blue. It became a defining mark of which families are more closely related. My family will always be strongly linked to all host families as we are the original family, but our closer host families maintain green chondria.

Even though Aiden and I are friends, I don't want him anywhere near Marley. "*What are you doing here, Aiden?*"

"*What? And let you have all the practice so you can beat me at this year's annual Gathering?"* Aiden thinks, sporting a huge grin.

Anna, of course, invited him to give me some competition. Well, fine, I'm up for it. *"Okay, you're on. But hands off my girlfriend, Marley, and I mean it."* I accentuate the last part slowly, hoping he takes me seriously.

"Oh, really? So there will be no prize then for the winner, eh? Well, I'm not going to promise you anything," he thinks, egging me on.

I know what he's trying to goad me into doing, and it isn't going to work. "Oh no, you don't. There is NO prize for this hunt. You better keep your eyes and hands to yourself around her, or you and I will have a serious problem," I say aloud, so he knows I mean every word.

Aiden seems to think and then alleges, rightfully so, "Oh I see. Well, then, why didn't you say that you were in love? My God, Will, you are completely smitten! Now I must meet this girl. Are we ready to begin?"

"I'm waiting for—" I start to think, but my cell phone chimes with a text message that reads, *On your mark, get set, GO!* from Anna.

"The quarry has been released. Good luck. You'll need it," I think right before I head off into the woods.

I lift my head, listening and smelling everything I can, to discern where the chipmunk is. Anna has driven quite a ways off as I barely detect the scent of the chipmunk. I won't be able to use my more valuable sense of touch until I get closer. My ears tell me the chipmunk is due east. I need to figure out a fast and less obvious route to her. Aiden will take the quickest route. So I need to take a different one in the hopes of stealing the chipmunk out from under him since he's physically faster than I am. My advantage over him is that I consider all obstacles instead of taking off in the most direct route. Beyond the stream I sensed, there is a very steep rock face to climb along the route Aiden has chosen. If I head a little to the north, I can bypass the stream and climb through a less imposing rocky area. I will lose about five minutes, but I could gain eight in the long run. It seems a smart choice, and I already know what Aiden has chosen.

An hour and a half later, I touch the ground at the top of a small cliff hang and immediately see in my mind that the chipmunk has crossed this path. I'm closing in, but sense Aiden doing the same. Anna placed her well, and it's been a challenge. The rocky area I climbed to the north was more difficult than I had originally thought. I wonder how steep it's been for Aiden to the south. Just as I'm about to climb down, I spot the chipmunk five hundred feet below. It's directly in front of me! She's foraging the ground by a dead tree lying across a path on the trail. I spot Aiden close by... to my left and on the ground eyeing her up, as well. He has the distance over me. I have no doubt in my mind he senses my closeness as I sense his.

My only chance is to jump down at exactly the right second...

AIDEN and I walk together through the woods in silence, and it's just as well. My mind is on the annual Gathering. My heart wasn't in the last few competitions, and Aiden's was. I've been feeling the weight of my First Tracker responsibilities for a long time. It's challenging enough to find potential hosts as all trackers do, but I also watch over other trackers and test them before awarding them their own onyx stones. I've given my stone to lots of potential hosts, but now that Marley has it, I don't think I ever want it back. Only my mom and I know the location of the original meteorite from which all tracker stones come from. This secrecy is something many hosts take issue with. Some hosts, Malcolm Durst included, think everyone should have access to the meteorite. But, my mom insists that the meteorite location needs to be kept a secret.

My biggest relief of duties happened when my Second Tracker, coincidentally, Aiden, was given the responsibility of training newbies. Each new tracker who is found must go through the proper training to understand and acclimate to their new enhanced senses. Aiden takes those responsibilities seriously during training sessions, but, as was recently evident with Dustin Kelly, he has problems following up with the trackers afterward. I can't blame Aiden too much, though. Dustin is a handful.

"So who are you dating now?"

Aiden laughs. "I don't kiss and tell, mate," he says with his ever-present grin. He's got a new girl on his arm almost every time I see him. Today is a rare exception. Anna must have warned him not to bring anyone.

"The ladies love you, man. I don't know how you do it; you aren't even one of the charismatic ones."

This isn't to say that I haven't had my fair share of girlfriends. The first time I met Sophia, now a South American tracker, we hit it off immediately. Well, at least she seemed to like me very much. There was also Lilah Durst, Malcolm's adopted host daughter. She's unbelievably beautiful, I'll give her that, but nasty as a snake. I only dated her for a few months, and I couldn't stand her. She was such a bitch to everyone, including me most of the time. Even though my mom was delighted that I was bridging a gap between a hostile host family and ours, I couldn't continue to date her.

In the end, I've never been able to see myself in a serious relationship with any of them...something was always missing. Now there's Marley, and nothing is missing. It's almost like my chondria chose for me. In any case, I'm feeling pretty lucky. It might have something to do with my win over Aiden this morning, or it could be my hot prom date. I grin at Aiden. "*Dude, you are screwed this year at the Gathering. I am on a roll!*"

"Keep dreamin', lover boy," Aiden jokes, pushing me.

We finally catch up with the girls. Anna is practicing no-touch archery. Marley is sitting on the grass watching. I approach Marley and reveal the chipmunk with a tiny little red ribbon around her foot. She looks at the chipmunk, a big smile on her face. I love her smile. It's so genuine. My chondria swirl around my irises. She asks a bunch of questions about how I tracked something so small. If she only knew......one year, the hunt judges selected a butterfly to track. Marley seems so intrigued with the chipmunk that she barely notices Aiden standing next to me. Until he speaks, of course.

"Aren't you something? You must be Marley," Aiden says with his magnetic nature, taking her hand, pushing me aside. What a show-off. His chondria are floating in his eyes intentionally, knowing how much girls like blue. Oh boy, here we go.

Marley says hello in response and asks Aiden about his chondria. They continue exchanging niceties, and I don't miss that she asks if he has a girlfriend, something I don't enjoy hearing. I shudder to think Marley might be interested in him. He's the ficklest host I've ever met. Don't get me wrong, he's a great friend. But I don't want him to be anywhere near *my* girl.

After the introductions, we leave to go have lunch at the Bellevue Diner. We grab a booth with one of those old tabletop jukeboxes. I've never seen anyone actually play one, but it's pretty cool to look at. After we order, Aiden tells stories about some of our past competitions. I can tell Aiden approves of Marley, and he thinks as much to me.

"You're one lucky bloke, Will. Does she have any friends?"

I shake my head at him, smiling. I am lucky, though, and it's been nice to take a break and have fun. That is, until something annoying happens.

There are a few boys sitting at a table across the restaurant from us, staring at Marley. They seem to know her. More importantly, I don't like the way one of the boys is looking at her or the way he's laughing with his buddies. Marley acknowledges the boy across the room with a wave, and her cheeks turn crimson.

"Do you know him?" I ask curiously.

"I think his name is John. He goes to Greencastle. I met him here once when I was out with Liz." Marley looks down at her hands, waiting for her cheeks to return to their normal color.

I take her hand in mine, squeezing in reassurance. When she smiles at me, I know what needs to be done. Once I see John and his friends get up to leave, I excuse myself, claiming to use the restroom and follow him and his friends outside.

"Hey, what was so funny inside?" I say to the boy walking away.

The boy stops and turns around. "What?"

Slowly, I walk over to him. "I said, what was so funny inside?"

John looks visibly nervous and glances at his two friends. "What's the problem? I was making a joke about that weird girl. She gave me her number once, but I was interested in her hot friend. What's it to you?" he asks, obviously gaining confidence because he's got his two buddies with him.

Stepping even closer, I think in my best impression of his voice, "*I'm a douchebag.*"

A look of confusion crosses his face.

I smile, knowingly.

"Let's get out of here, guys," he says, shifting uncomfortably. He turns and walks quickly to his car. His friends stand there looking at each other.

"Guys, let's go!" John yells, already in the driver's seat.

"See ya around," I say before walking back toward the diner. Good, problem solved. I return to the booth with a smile on my face and an approving look from Anna and Aiden.

Sitting in the back of the car with Marley after lunch, I reach for her hand. She smiles. We're heading back to my house for Marley to meet my dad for the first time. We sit in silence, me caressing circles with my finger in her palm. Every time she looks at me, my chondria push me closer to her. That's the one thing about being a host, chondria enhance our feelings, and there's one thing I know for certain. I'm falling in love with Marley Hunter.

Marley

Robert Reed is the most charismatic man I've ever met in my life. From the moment I place my hand in his, I know he's special. He's a little shorter than Will with light brown hair and eyes that remind me of chocolate. I certainly feel like melted chocolate as I remove my hand from his.

"It's very nice to finally meet you, Marley. Will has told me so much about you. Please come in and have a seat," Mr. Reed says, motioning me inside his house.

"Thank you, Mr. Reed," I manage, feeling strangely at ease.

He smiles. "Oh no, please call me Robert."

Will puts his arm around me, guiding me into his living room, while Aiden and Anna take off to somewhere else in the house. I'm struck by the beauty of the Reeds' house. I would guess they hired an interior decorator based on the vibrant green and tan color scheme, an abundance of pillows, and pictures adorning the walls. Will pulls me down next to him on a very plush white and tan striped sofa. I sink into the cushions wondering if I'll be able to get back up. Robert sits down in a chair next to me.

"Marley, I want to apologize that my wife, Jane, isn't here to meet you. She's away on an important trip," Robert says, voice dripping with honey.

"Oh, that's okay." Honestly, I'm relieved that I don't have to face Will's mom yet. Her psychic abilities are going to make me really nervous. My biggest fear is that she will sense that I have no special ability and that I'll make a weak host.

Robert smiles as if he senses my trepidation, and the nervousness dissipates. Instead, I can't help but mirror his smile. He's so pleasant and happy.

"So tell me, what do you think of us? I imagine it's been a lot to take in."

"Come on, Dad. You just met her. Don't get all personal, okay?" Will says, protectively.

Normally I'd be uncomfortable being put on the spot like this, but not with Robert. It's that voice in my head telling me, "*You can trust him.*"

"It's okay, I don't mind," I say to Will and then turn back to Robert. "Well, yeah, at first it was overwhelming. Now I think it's fascinating. The abilities, the thoughts, the dreams..." I stop mid-thought, blushing because of the dreams I have with Will. "What I mean is...I think it's all very amazing."

"I'm so glad you feel that way. We work very hard to be the best we can." Robert seems to consider something and thinks to me, "*Marley, would you mind if I ask Will to leave so we can have a moment alone?*"

His voice in my head is startling, but it sounds as rich and soothing as when he speaks aloud. I nod. "Sure."

There's silence for a moment, and I can tell Robert is thinking to Will. Will shakes his head but seems to acquiesce in the end. Before he stands, he leans over and gives me a quick hug. "*I'm sorry, my dad is...just like this. I'll be in the kitchen if you need me.*"

Once Will is gone, I look back at Robert.

"I trust Will told you about some of the government regulations we have to follow and our need for secrecy?"

"Yes, he did," I reply, not sure where this is going.

"How are you feeling about your family then? If you choose to host, you will eventually have to break ties with them. Even though we hide well, living closely with non-hosts is dangerous. The government will not allow us to risk exposure, at least not yet. Some teenagers like you wait until they graduate from high school, and a few even wait until they graduate from college. We don't have many opportunities to find potential hosts, so sometimes we have to recruit those who are younger."

It's like he knows exactly what my concerns are about hosting. I feel so at ease with him that I can't help but be completely honest. "It's upsetting to think about losing my mom and stepdad, Ray. I'm not sure how I could cope with that. It's scary thinking about being on my own without them. Plus, my mom lost my dad before I was born. I don't think she could take thinking I was gone too." A lump forms in my throat. I swallow, refusing to give into sadness.

Robert moves to the sofa and sits down next to me. "It can be gradual, Marley. I want you to know that, if you decide to host, you will never be alone. I'd love nothing more than to have you as part of my family. I see the way Will looks at you. I knew as soon as I opened that door that you were special, especially to him."

Tears prick at the corners of my eyes. I don't know if it's his special ability, or that he's a kind man, but I can't help myself. I hug him. "Thank you."

"It's a shame not everyone can host chondria. Believe me, we're working on that very thing," he says soothingly, giving my shoulders one last squeeze.

"Will is lucky to have a dad like you."

"Yes, I am. Am I allowed back in here now?" Will asks, cautiously.

Robert smiles at me. "Of course, son. She's a wonderful girl."

After saying goodbye, Will drives me home. I'm still floating from talking with Robert and can't seem to stop the calm euphoria. Will jokes about how his dad always makes people feel so relaxed.

Um, yeah...does he ever.

18

PRELUDE

Marley

It's the day of the prom.

I stretch my arms above my head lazily, lying in bed. It is, after all, a Saturday. Plus, last night I dreamt with Will. He took me to the private island he showed me weeks ago when we first met. The sand felt warm and soft under my feet, and the water was a beautiful cerulean. Tiny fish swam beneath the surface. After a swim, we sat on the sand as the waves lapped at our legs, talking about our lives and hopes for the future.

I ought to get up since tonight is kind of a big night. My mom comes into my room, disrupting my thoughts, bright-eyed and happy.

"Time to get ready for your prom, Marley!" she exclaims, excitement oozing out of every syllable. She goes into my closet to fish out my dress.

I respond through a yawn, "Morning. Mom. I'm not getting dressed yet. I have like eight hours, you know."

She emerges from my closet, my dress over her arm, rolling her eyes. "Oh, Marley, I know that." She brushes her hand across the fabric, admiringly. "I want to get it out and see if it needs a steaming for wrinkles. It really is a beautiful dress." She touches the tiny little flowers sewn on the top. "I remember my prom like it was yesterday. Your dad picked me up in his old vintage black Camaro. He worked on that car himself. He borrowed his father's tuxedo, and I wore pink. That was the night I knew he was the one..." Her voice is dreamy as she reminisces.

I've heard this story tons of times. A year after they went to the prom, they graduated, got married, and my dad went overseas in the military. At the time, my dad didn't even know that my mom was pregnant with me. I should have known she would be thinking about him today.

"Oh, Mom, I'm not moving out or anything." I get out of bed to give her a hug. "Let's try to minimize the tears today, okay?"

She smiles. "Yes, yes, of course." She wipes away a single tear and comes back to the present. "How about some breakfast?"

Will

She's in her room in the attic. I can hear her pacing unsteadily in her heels. The distinct swishing of fabric moving back and forth tells me she's in front of a mirror. She must look beautiful, I think, pulling the emergency brake. I reach for Marley's corsage and step out of my car. My first instinct is to glance up at one of Marley's fan windows.

As if on cue, she's there in the window peering down at

me. Startled by seeing me, she ducks out of sight. I can't help but smile. She's nervous. Well, that's a good thing. I walk up the pathway to the front door. After one last check of my tuxedo, making sure everything is in order, I ring the doorbell.

Inside, Marley's mom yells, "Marley, Will's here." Then she's opening the door.

She looks me up and down and smiles, approvingly. "Well, look at you. Very handsome, Will."

I smile in kind. "Thank you, Mrs. Jensen."

"Well, come on in. I'd like to snap a few photos of the two of you out back, if you don't mind."

"No, that would be great. Is Marley ready?" I ask, getting a little nervous about the lack of footsteps on the stairs. She's still up in her room.

"*I'm sure you look great,*" I think to her, hoping to give her confidence.

I hear her inhale quickly, clearly surprised to hear my voice. A few seconds later the sound of heels click on the wooden steps leading from her room to the second floor.

I let go of the breath I was holding and train my eyes on the steps.

The first thing I see is a swish of purple grazing the tips of polished toes. Then, I see all of her, and she's stunning, breathtaking even. My lips part in awe. From her swept up straightened hair to her dress, baring her beautiful neck and shoulders, she's absolutely gorgeous.

I'm speechless. Literally, I can't say anything. My chondria are bouncing around inside my chest uncontrollably. I've never experienced anything like this before; it's like they feel the same way I do about her. My first instinct is to bend over, hands on my knees, and take a few deep breaths, but that would seem extremely odd. Instead, I barely move and try to take control back. *"Calm down,"* I think inwardly.

Marley's parents tell her that she looks very pretty, and a long pause follows. It's my turn. *Come on, Will.*

She glances down and fidgets.

Say something, you idiot!

"You are...beautiful," I say slowly, hoping my chondria won't betray me and fill my eyes.

Marley looks back up. "Thanks. My mom and Anna helped me pick out the dress." Her eyes dart sideways, clearly disappointed in her own response. "You look great too. The tuxedo suits you."

Marley's mom beams. "I think I might cry." She grabs a camera from the table. "But, before that starts happening, let's get some pictures of you two on the patio."

We head out back, and Marley's mom takes a few pictures as Marley smiles uncomfortably. Then we are out the door and on our way to the prom. As we drive off, I take her hand in mine. *"You look incredible tonight. I can't believe how lucky I am that you agreed to go to the prom with me."*

"Thanks, I wasn't sure how I would turn out. My mom helped. I never knew my hair could be this straight. Oh, and I asked you, remember?"

I laugh. "How could I forget?"

I put on some music, and she leans back into the passenger seat. I'm taking the long way to the country club, where our prom is being held. I could use some time to steady myself before the main event. I don't mind being around people. In fact, I enjoy it most of the time. But the effect she has on me is making my chondria behave abnormally. The last thing I need right now is an entire room of teenagers to see my eyes lit up.

I glance over at her. She's mulling something over in her head. I can tell by the way she keeps drawing in her bottom lip in with her teeth. "What are you thinking?" I ask, glancing back and forth from her to the road.

"Just that my mom did so much for me today. She was really excited for me to go to prom. I don't know. What will I do without her if I decide to host?"

I knew this would come up eventually. She has a close relationship with her mom. "Don't worry, Marley, I'll be with you," I say, hoping to ease her pain.

"Are you freakin' kidding me? You did not just say that."

"Wait... what's wrong?"

"Look, I get that you want me to be a host, but you have a mom, and you get to keep her. I would have to give mine up. Do you understand how hard that will be for me? I didn't have a dad when I was young, but I had a mom, and she was great. She's always put me first in everything, and she's about the best mom ever. So don't flippantly tell me that I'll have you as if my mom can be replaced so easily."

One look at her and I know she's serious. What the hell? That was not at all what I meant! I pull over to the side of the road and turn off the car.

I turn toward her, feeling both hurt and shocked that she would think I don't care about her relationship with her mom and that my only interest in her is to make her a host. I may be a lot of things, but I would never manipulate anyone into becoming a host. "I'm sorry that I'm asking you to give up your mom, I know that you have a special relationship with her. I'm sorry if I came off as a jerk. I didn't mean to. If you don't want to be a host, I'll have to accept that."

She looks down at her lap, her cheeks flaming up. Why is she so upset?

"Will, I'm sorry. I shouldn't have said all that. I've been so freaked out about all of this. I mean, first everyone is congratulating me for dating you, then you tell me I can be like you, then to top it all off, I have to give up my parents."

I feel terrible about her dilemma. I say the only thing I can think of to help. "But, you're special, Marley."

She throws her hands in the air. "God, Will! That's it, isn't it? I'm only in this position because my DNA is compatible with chondria."

It hurts, but she's right. She's in this position because of her DNA. I look out the window at the tree line. Maybe I shouldn't have spent so much time with her. Maybe she doesn't want to be a host. Did I sense that somehow? *Am* I manipulating her?

"Hey, I'm not faking my attraction toward you because I want you to become a host. You know that, right?"

"Do I?" she asks, inhaling sharply. "Look, I don't know. Maybe I'm being crazy here. Maybe the stress of this huge life decision is getting to me. I'm sorry if I've ruined our night. God, I feel like such an idiot! You're probably so pissed right now."

"Actually, you look kind of amazing."

She rolls her eyes. "Yeah, right. I'm like on the verge of a nervous breakdown. I doubt I look amazing."

Is she crazy? I can barely resist being this close to her! "No, I don't know what you mean. I've never met anyone more irresistible than you. You look beautiful tonight. Plus, do you have any idea how incredible you look without your clothes on?"

She looks up and hits my arm in mock anger and shock. "I still can't believe you saw me in that ravine! You're such a perv!"

"*So does this count as our first fight as a couple?*" I think, putting my hand under her chin, turning her face toward mine, my chondria swirling in my eyes.

She smiles, seeming to let her anxiety about her decision go. "I guess." Then as an afterthought, she asks, "So when do I get to see you without *your* clothes on?"

My first thought is to skip prom. Instead, I smile and wink. "We'd better get going."

WE PULL into the parking lot of the country club, and Marley reaches for the door handle. Instantly, I grab her hand.

"Hold on," I say, looking around the parking lot, scanning. Something isn't right. There's someone here.

"What's up? Is there something wrong?" she asks anxiously, looking around the parking lot too.

Without looking at her, I think, "*I need to scan the area. I sense another host nearby.*"

I block out all other sounds and concentrate on what my chondria are sensing. "*Who's out there?*"

Nothing.

Then I hear, "*It's me, Will.*"

I sigh, falling back against my seat, relieved and turn to Marley.

"Up for meeting a friend?"

Marley peers out the windows. "Seriously? Who's the friend?"

I should prepare her. I don't want her to be taken by surprise. *"Parker West and his family are visiting from California. There is a doctor here who may be able to help his son. They are also very close friends of my family. He stopped by here to say hello and give me a message, I believe."*

"Okay, so where is he?"

"Hang on, I should warn you, Parker's special gift...."

Before I can explain what the special gift is, her door opens, and Parker is pulling her out of the car. I know that as soon as he touches her, she will feel instantly warm all over. It's very annoying. I get out and round the car quickly.

Parker is admiring Marley. "Wow, Will, you certainly have a beauty here," he says, smiling brilliantly.

I'm by Marley's side instantly, putting my arm around her. "This is my friend, Parker. He was very charming before he became a host. Now he's positively unbearable." I remove her hand from Parker's.

Marley's dazed and confused, and can't look away from Parker. I roll my eyes. I can't stand her looking at him this way. Granted, Parker is a good-looking guy. He's got light blond hair and blue eyes, and one of those California tans. He's in perfect shape, a perfect smile, a perfect everything. In fact, he might as well be carved out of stone.

I squeeze her hand. *"I know. It's unsettling. Give yourself a minute to recover."* Without realizing that I'm still thinking to her, I add, *"Then you can remember that you're MY girlfriend."* Oh shit. *"Sorry, I didn't mean for you to hear that."*

It doesn't matter, though; I can tell my thoughts are barely making a dent. She's completely mesmerized by Parker.

"Dude! Could you ease up, please? She's my girlfriend!"

His eyes never leave Marley's. *"Chill out, Will. You've really got it bad for this one."*

After what seems like forever, Marley finally speaks. "I...I...I, um, what I mean is, it's nice to meet you, Parker."

Parker smiles, bowing. "The pleasure is all mine." Then to me, "I don't want to interrupt your evening, but I do need to speak with you briefly."

"What's this about?"

"I'm not the only host nearby."

"I'm on guard."

Marley interrupts our thoughts. "Okay, well, I'm sure Liz and Becca are here already, I'll go and find them." She looks up at me. "You'll come and find me when you're finished talking to Parker?"

I glance at Parker. "Can't this wait? I don't want Marley walking into the prom without me."

Before Parker can answer, she interjects, "No, Will, it's fine. Parker clearly has something important to tell you, and I could use a little recovery time after the uh...handshake?" She blushes, nodding at Parker.

"She's a gem," Parker affirms.

I turn her toward me and put my arms around her waist. "I won't be more than a few minutes. I'm sorry about this, and I promise I will make it up to you." I kiss her in front of Parker and everyone else in the parking lot. After we part, my eyes follow her all the way to the front door of the country club. Once she's inside, I turn my attention back to Parker.

"Who else do you sense nearby?"

"I don't know who it is, but he's strong." His eyes are serious.

"Malcolm?"

"*No, I didn't sense him. It's someone else. But, Will, Malcolm has a way of using others if you know what I mean?*"

"*I know that, but I've been on guard. I'm watching her closely. My senses are the best of our kind, and I have no intention of letting anyone near her. I think she's getting close to making a decision, so it won't be much longer.*"

"*That's fine, but you've got it bad for her. What if she chooses not to host? Even if we erase her memories of you, Malcolm already knows about her. What if he makes an attempt for her?*"

The thought of Marley not wanting to be a host is devastating. I push the thought from my mind. "*I can't think about Marley's choice right now. But the one thing I know for sure is that Malcolm is only interested in what I'm interested in, and you know why. So, if Marley does decide not to host, I will move on immediately. Malcolm will follow suit.*"

Parker shrugs his shoulders reluctantly. "*If you say so...*"

"*Now, can I get back to my date and prom?*"

"*Haven't you been to enough proms?*" Parker asks, his brilliant smile returning.

I grin. "*None like this one.*"

I turn and walk toward the entrance to the country club and Marley, the thoughts of Malcolm dissipating rapidly.

19

THE MAIN EVENT

Marley

I wander into the front of the country club lobby, looking for a sign. Which room is our prom being held in? I've never been here before, but the chandeliers and wainscoting feel like old money. Becca's here all the time for dinner with her parents. Her father golfs here when he isn't doing lawyer stuff. Everywhere I look I see ornate furniture and, glancing up, chandeliers hanging in the halls leading away from the entrance. There's an easel with a sign set up beside a cream-colored loveseat with cherry wood clawed feet. As my eyes focus on the words on the sign, someone taps my shoulder. I jump, startled.

"Hey, girl! You look incredible!" Liz says with a toothy grin. "What do you think of my dress?" She twirls around, her arms outstretched.

She could have worn a paper bag and looked great, but tonight she's wearing a short red sequin dress that showcases all of her great assets. "You look terrific, Liz." I hug her and tilt my head to look behind her. "Where's Mike?"

"He's inside already, I just came back from checking my makeup in the bathroom." Now it's her turn to look behind me. "Where's *your* date, Marley? He didn't stand you up, did he?" Her eyes turn to slits as she continues, "That jerk. I'll kill him—"

"Calm down. He's here. He's parking the car," I interrupt, not wanting her to know what he's doing, and a little irritated that she thinks I've been stood up.

Liz puts her hand over her mouth in embarrassment. "Sorry, I shouldn't have said that. Of course he's here. It's only that you're my best friend, ya know?" She looks so remorseful that I can't be mad at her...especially on a night like tonight.

"No biggie. Let's go. Is Becca here too?"

Liz smiles. "Yep, she's inside with...." Suddenly the smile is replaced with concern. "Um, we're sitting with Will's sister, Anna, too. Do you think your date will mind?"

"No, that's cool. Will likes his sister. I just don't know how Anna is going to deal with her date, Mr. Penn State." I imagine Anna getting so annoyed by A.J.'s constant talk of football that she picks him up with her special ability and throws him. We look at each other and burst out laughing. If she only knew what I was actually thinking...

Once she composes herself, Liz's expression turns serious. "So listen, I think that Mike is going to be the prom king, or at least that's what everyone keeps telling me. Do you think I'll be prom queen? It would be way too embarrassing if he wins and I don't, since we're a couple. What do you think? Am I being ridiculous?"

Are you serious? I scowl silently because I can see she's

truly anxious about this, something I rarely see from her. I can't imagine anyone being worried about a prom queen contest. "Liz, you're the only girl at this prom who has a shot at winning. If anything, my date might give Mike a run for his money." I'm half-joking, but there might be some truth to it.

"Really? You think Will might be prom king? But he's new at our school. I seriously doubt it."

I shrug my shoulders. "Hey, what do I know? Can we go to our prom now? I'm starving."

Liz's smile returns. "Me too. Let's go."

As I walk into the ballroom allotted to Pine Grove Junior Prom, the first thing I notice is all the silver and gold balloons scattered across the dance floor and floating above us on the ceiling. They put matching streamers all over the ceiling and walls. I'm happy to see the prom committee went with a DJ, who's perched up on a stage below a sign that reads, *Welcome Pine Grove High Juniors*. Classical music hits my ears, and it feels like I thought prom would.

Liz points over to one of the many white linen-covered tables adorned with gold and silver confetti in the corner. Most of the other tables are already filled with classmates. I spot Becca, her boyfriend, Henry, who goes to Shippensburg High, Anna, A.J., and Mike. They look pretty happy. I should be happy too, except that I can't help but think my date should be here with me. I wonder what Parker is telling Will, and if it has anything to do with me. What's keeping him?

Just then someone taps me on the shoulder. I turn, hoping to see Will, but it's Justin. Whoa! He looks amazing in his black tuxedo. I've never seen him in anything but his tan pants and boring shirts. His hair is gelled, and his face is clean-shaven. He smiles. "Good evening, ladies. Marley, you look beautiful tonight. Will you save me a dance?"

"Justin, you look so different..." I say, unable to string my words together; I'm so taken aback by his physical transformation. "Um, sure."

Liz smiles at him too. "Well, hello there, Mr. McSteamy. Who are you here with then?"

"I'm alone tonight, but hopeful." He smiles playfully with an air of confidence, then winks at us both.

Liz laughs and pats Justin on the arm. "I'm going to go sit with my date. See you at the table, Marley. Have fun, Justin." She winks back before she walks away.

I smile at Justin, happy that my friend has finally returned to me, although he isn't exactly the same; tonight he's downright hot. I'm about to say something about that when his face changes from congenial to sour. Uh-oh. Before I can even turn around to glance at the door, Will is there behind me.

He puts his chin on my shoulder. "*I'm sorry it took so long. I won't leave your side for the rest of the night. Please forgive me.*"

It feels good to be close to Will, but I also know Justin doesn't like him. Abruptly I move to the side. "Hey, Will, do you know my friend, Justin Jameson?"

They nod to one another and Will smiles. "Yeah, I think we met in the nurse's office a while back. Good to see you." I can tell Will is cautious, but trying to be friendly.

Justin doesn't smile; instead, he frowns. "Yeah, that's right. I hope you know how lucky you are to be here with her. She's a really great girl. You two have a nice dinner, and Marley, don't forget that dance."

I manage to nod and watch him walk away. Hmm, great girl? He's still acting strangely. I turn back to Will.

"I see that I shouldn't leave you alone for even a second. Am I forgiven for allowing you to walk into our prom by yourself?" He has the cutest sad face I've ever seen.

I reach out and pull his arms around my waist. I won't ever be able to stay mad at him for long. I graze his cheek with mine, and whisper, "You're forgiven."

The dinner consisted of roast chicken with mixed vegetables, a twice-baked potato, and chocolate cake for dessert. I swear Anna put her hand out for the pepper shaker just out of reach, but somehow managed to grasp it. Will gives her a reprimanding look, and she smiles. They have such a great relationship; it makes me a little sad that I don't have a sibling.

As we eat, we laugh about our latest home-ec debacle. It was supposed to be some type of chicken casserole with a brown crust. It ended up being a casserole with uncooked white goop on top. A.J. and Mike had eaten some of it and said it was decent. Liz, Becca, and I had no desire to give it a try. Most of our disasters in class happen because one of the boys mixes something up.

It feels good to not be the single person tagging along anymore. I look at Will so many times, afraid he might vanish. At one point, he thinks to me, *"Are you okay?"* I blush and nod. He must think I'm being weird. I've got to stop watching him. Still, it means a lot that he's here and that I'm actually attending prom. One month earlier I was planning on spending the evening watching movies at home with Mom and Ray.

After a while, the DJ starts playing some music we can

dance to. I love to dance. I didn't talk to Will about this beforehand, so I have no clue if he does too. Some guys at school never dance at school functions. What if Will is one of those guys? Oh, what the hell? "Want to dance?"

He smiles. "Sweet. I was just about to ask you."

He takes my hand as we walk to the dance floor. We dance for a few fast songs, and I'm impressed. "Where did you learn to dance?"

"I've had tons of practice. My mom likes dancing. She makes me partner with her all the time at the Annual Host Gathering." For the very first time, Will blushes. It may be the sexiest thing I've ever seen.

"Will Reed, you're blushing!"

The music stops, and we turn and look at the stage. Mr. Graham, our home-ec teacher, is walking toward the microphone. He announces that the prom king and queen are going to be crowned momentarily, and we should all gather on the dance floor. I spot Liz and Mike and wave them over to us. Okay, here's Liz's big moment. I hope she and Mike win. I actually feel a little nervous for her. I hug her and whisper in her ear, "You got this."

"Thanks, friend."

Will, who is standing on my other side, squeezes my hand. I look up at him as he thinks, *"You should know, I voted for you."*

"You're crazy," I say, rolling my eyes. "Don't be mad, but I didn't vote for you. I voted for Liz and Mike. Sorry," I tease, squeezing his hand back.

Mr. Graham approaches the microphone again with two envelopes. "Here we go. The Pine Grove Junior Prom Queen is..." He breaks the seal on one of the envelopes, pulling out a slip of paper. "Liz Larson."

The crowd on the dance floor erupts in applause. I hug her again and push her toward the stage. I'm so happy for her. Once she reaches Mr. Graham, he puts a crown on her head as she waves to everyone.

Mr. Graham goes back to the microphone again and says, "And now the Pine Grove Junior Prom King is..." He opens the second envelope. "Will Reed."

"*What?*" Will thinks so loudly it hurts my head. Our whole class applauds, except for Liz and Mike. I understand why, but on the other hand, I don't mind at all. The shock and embarrassment on his face is totally worth it. I clap and push him forward. Based on his expression when he reaches the stage, he's still in shock. I smile up at him and Liz—my two favorite people. Then Mr. Graham announces that the king and queen will have a dance to themselves. Liz and Will smile awkwardly at each other and head to the dance floor.

As soon as they start dancing, I notice a very gloomy Mike. "Hey, come on, Mike. It's no big deal. It's a stupid contest. She's here with you, right?"

"I know, it's just that Will is so popular now, and well... look at them. They look like the perfect couple. I can't compete with that," Mike says, emotionally beaten. Then, as if remembering that he's talking about my boyfriend (yes, I said it—*my* boyfriend), he adds, "No offense or anything."

I realize there's some truth to what Mike said. When I look at Will and Liz dancing, I'm struck by how perfect they really do look together. Clearly, they're a very attractive pair. But I'm not worried in the slightest because I know for a fact that Will isn't interested in Liz. He's into me. Poor Mike. Boys can be so dense sometimes.

"Say listen, Mike, Liz is lucky to have a guy like you. If you don't mind dancing with me..." I offer, trying to lift his spirits and minimize how crummy he must be feeling.

He looks at me as if he's noticing me for the very first time, maybe shocked at my invitation to dance. After a small pause, he replies, "Sure, why not? Let's show 'em how it's done."

Mike reaches out his hand and twirls me around a few times before placing his hand on the small of my back. I laugh and glance over at Will and Liz.

Will smiles at me. *You better save the next dance for me.*

I return his smile. Then, as if all the air is somehow sucked out of the room, something odd happens. Will's smile fades into something serious, and I think his eyes glow. He looks back at me, shaking his head. The glow is gone, but the feeling I have remains. Something is off. I wonder what he's thinking, and if he will tell me about it.

The song ends, and Mike lets go of me. He doesn't let go of my hand, though. "What's up, Mike?"

"Why Will?"

"What do you mean?"

"I mean, why did you pick Will to date? Liz and I set you up with a few of my cousins, and Justin Jameson has been like totally in love with you since the moment he met you. So why Will?"

Hey, let's get really personal, why don't we? "Well..." I start, not sure how to put it. "I connect with Will. He gets me in a way that no one else does, and I think I get him." I shrug my shoulders. Then, as an afterthought, I add, "By the way, I don't think Justin is in love with me, we're just friends."

Mike seems to think about what I've said. "Well, if I've ever heard of a good reason to date someone, I guess that would be it. Hey, if it doesn't work out with Will, there's always Justin, who, whether you see it or not, *is* in love with you, Marley. Laters." And he's gone to go dance with Liz.

What the hell? I'm feeling downright dense and oblivious and want nothing more than to find a private place to mull this over. Before I can get off the dance floor, Justin is in front of me, taking my hand, pulling me close to him. Oh, I forgot that I promised him a dance. After a few moments of dancing in silence, I look up at him and realize what Mike said is true. Quickly I look back down, trying to avoid a conversation. That explains why he doesn't like Will. Oh no, this isn't good. Why didn't I see it? It all makes sense. I'm such a fool to have not seen it. Have I been leading him on?

The song ends, and as he opens his mouth to say something, I interrupt, "Hey listen, Justin, you're an awesome friend, thanks for the dance." I walk away, looking for Will, feeling guilty for something I didn't even know I did.

My mind is spinning about Justin when Will's arms surround me again. The music is still slow as he takes my hand, puts his other hand on my waist, and draws me close. *"Now this is my favorite kind of dancing, and you are my favorite person."*

It feels good to be in his arms, allowing all the guilt about Justin to wash completely away. My feelings are for Will. I rest my head on his shoulder, wishing I could speak to him through my thoughts the way he can to me. Wait a minute; I can have that if I want. I'm a potential host. I've thought of all the different angles, and my biggest issue is my mom and Ray. I love them, but they would want me to be happy.

I still haven't made a decision. If I choose Will, I will never see my parents again. If I choose my parents, I never see Will again. This blows.

Will senses my apprehension and pulls back to search my eyes. A few chondria floating around in his irises are making them glow like fireflies in a field at dusk. "What are you thinking?"

I find myself lost in his eyes, unable to respond. I'm a little scared but know I shouldn't be. Instinctively, I reach up and touch his cheek.

His eyes lose focus, and he places his hand on my cheek. Whoa, what's going on? The next thing I know, the ballroom disappears, and it's only the two of us surrounded by a dark sky filled with stars. "Will, what's happening?" I ask, aware that the event is happening to both of us.

"I don't know," he responds slowly, still unfocused. He kisses my forehead first and then moves his lips down across my skin toward my cheek, sending sparks along my skin.

My breath catches, and tears pool in my eyes as if I should somehow be feeling sad. What's the matter with me? Why do I feel this way? The sorrow quickly turns to panic, and I'm blasted back to the present, the ballroom around me returning. I don't know what makes me say what I say next, but I do it anyway.

"I have to go to the bathroom."

20

ALL GOOD THINGS...

Marley

I leave Will standing on the dance floor as I pick up the skirt to my dress and hurry into the foyer of the country club. I'm so confused and need some air. What *was* that between us? It was like we weren't ourselves, but we were. I have to catch my breath and calm down. I look up and down the hallway for some sign of where the bathrooms are when Tori Lewis taps me on the shoulder, making me jump.

"Oh...sorry, Marley, I didn't mean to scare you. Can I ask you a favor? There's a line for the bathroom on this side. Come with me to the one on the other side of the club?"

She looks pretty in her hot pink dress and pumps to match, but she doesn't look too happy. I wonder what's up.

I manage a small smile. "Oh hi, Tori. Um, sure. Do you know where they are?" I ask, looking up and down the hall again.

"Sure, I've been here before with Joe's parents. I'll show you," she responds, her tone seeming ominous.

"Okay..." I reply hesitantly as I follow her down the hall. She looks like she's been crying and then touched up her makeup. There are still smudges under her eyes, and the tip of her nose is a little red. She's obviously not having a good evening. I wonder if her douchebag boyfriend, Joe, has something to do with it.

"Tori, are you okay?"

She mumbles something inaudible under her breath, and then replies in the same gloomy voice, "I just need a break from all the excitement." She isn't looking at me anymore, and she is starting to weird me out.

The other side of the club seems to be shut down for the evening. Only a few dimmed lights illuminate the halls. It's actually kind of creepy. "Tori, are you sure we're allowed over here?"

"Yeah, it's fine."

God, she's acting so bizarre. When we reach the ladies' room, she opens the door for me. I pass her into the bathroom. Instead of following me, she slams the door in my face! She presses against the door. I grab the door knob and push. I can't open the door with her putting all her weight against it.

I bang on the door. "Hey, Tori? What're you doing? Open the door!" *What the hell is going on?* "Tori!"

"I'm...sorry, Marley...I had no choice." Then I hear something being lodged under the doorknob.

I ball my hands into fists and bang harder on the door. "Had no choice? What do you mean you had no choice?" My mind whirls, trying to figure out what she's talking about. What reason would Tori Lewis have to lock me in a bathroom at our prom? This is nuts.

Tori's voice interrupts my banging. "The guy in the

parking lot...he has Joe out there. He told me that I had to lock you in this bathroom if I ever want to see him again. I'm so sorry, Marley. I know no one thinks he's worth it, but Joe means everything to me."

I press my palms to the door, pleading. "Tori? Listen to me. You have to let me out. I can help you with Joe...please don't leave me in here." I have to stay calm.

I wait for her to respond. Nothing.

"Tori!"

Still nothing.

Slowly, I twist my body around to face the room. Don't freak out. Don't...oh shit! I can't believe this is happening! Why the hell did I leave Will on the dance floor? Does he know that I'm in trouble? Focus. This is no time for *what if's*!

My eyes slowly scan the room. I'm in a powder room with a row of cushioned stools, a sandy marble countertop, and a long mirror framed with soft, round light bulbs as I would imagine on a movie set. To my left is another door. It must lead to sinks and toilet stalls. Okay, take a deep breath. Maybe there's another girl in here? Cautiously, I creep to the door leading to the toilets and sinks.

"Hello? Is anyone in there?" I'm trying not to sound desperate, but who am I kidding?

My breathing increases as claustrophobia takes over. The walls seem to close in on me. I take a few deep breaths, trying to settle my nerves. I've got bigger things to worry about. Based on what Tori said, someone is most likely coming to get me. I need to be ready. As I look around for something I can use as a weapon, I hear a stall door open and slam shut. It's so loud that I know it isn't another girl using the restroom. I begin backing up to the outside door. There is a moment, no a *second*, when a person realizes that something really bad is about to happen, and panic sets in. My pulse picks up, and I can't catch my breath. I suspect the cause of my intense anxiety is about to rear its ugly head.

The bathroom door swings open, and the scariest-looking person I've ever seen walks into the powder room. His eyes glow, but not the beautiful green firefly lights I see in Will's eyes. Rather, his eyes are glowing hazily, like a photo does when you have poor lighting. They are eerie and listless with a purplish tint. His hair is dark and greasy, and the smell of sweat and B.O. gags me as it hits my nostrils. Oh God, don't vomit. He's wearing a filthy pair of sweatshorts and a yellowed white tank top. His muscles are massive, and I know it won't be much of a fight.

What's happened to him? He stares at me and raises his head, sniffing the air. What's he doing? Can he even see? Maybe, if I'm quiet, he won't see me. As he moves forward with rope in his hand, I realize I don't have a prayer. He knows exactly where I am. I have nowhere to go, and even if the door was unlocked, there's no way I would make it in time. I start to scream as he reaches for me. It's too late. He's already overpowering me, covering my mouth. The last thing I remember thinking is, *why didn't I bring Will's stone with me?*

I REGAIN CONSCIOUSNESS, and I can't move. As my eyes focus, I realize I'm in the back of some type of utility van with my wrists and ankles bound with rope. My first instinct is to scream for help, but no sound comes out because there's something in my mouth. I begin to hyperventilate, my chest heaving. The gag is choking me. A voice inside my head says, *"Calm down. Stop struggling."*

Slowly, I take a breath. In and out. In and out. Slower. In and out. I do this for a few minutes until my breathing is under control. What happened? Why am I tied up in the back of a van? My head spins, and my arms, pulled behind my back, are killing me. I retrace my steps... prom...Will... dancing...what happened next? I can't think, so I stop again. Breathe. In and out. In and out. What happened? The bathroom. Tori. Oh no, I remember...the boy with ugly glowing eyes. What does he want with me?

Oh my God! This is because of Will! My heart begins to pound so hard I think it might explode as I wonder what he's going to do with me.

I look around for something to use as a weapon. Not that it would do any good since my arms are tied behind my back, but I'm in serious panic mode. I keep hearing Agent Rushmore's voice in my head, *"You are in danger, you are in danger, you are in danger..."*

I have no idea how much time passes but after what seems like forever, the van pulls onto a road of stones. The crunching noise under the tires is unmistakable. I don't think I can stay like this much longer. I've lost feeling in my hands, and my shoulders are on fire. *Please get me out of here. I don't care what happens; just get me out of here!* I hold my breath as I hear the squeak of brakes as the van comes to a stop.

Will

I scan the crowd and realize it's been fifteen minutes since Marley left to use the restroom. I have no idea what happened. I lost control somehow. I remember dancing with Marley and then she said she had to use the restroom. What did I say? Did I offend her? Scare her? I must have done something since she hasn't come back. Looking down at my watch again, I decide to wait for her outside the restrooms. What the hell happened? I've never lost complete control like this before.

I walk quickly to the ladies' room and realize I can't simply walk in. I turn back around frustrated. Finally, I see Marley's friend Becca walking toward me.

"Um, hey, Becca, I don't suppose you would mind seeing how Marley is? She went to the bathroom a while ago, and I think she might be upset."

Becca frowns. "Oh no. Do you know why she's upset?"

Yeah, she's freaked out because I blacked out and somehow said something awful to her! Instead, I reply, "I'm not entirely sure, but could you check on her, please? I'm getting worried."

Becca must see my desperation because she nods and quickly goes into the bathroom. I start pacing in front of the door. What did I say to her? How did I lose control like that? I've been searching a long time for someone like her, and I may have somehow screwed it all up. What if she is sick or something? And what is taking Becca so long?

Becca emerges from the bathroom. "Sorry, Will, but Marley isn't in the bathroom. Maybe she's back in the ballroom?"

My heart stops. No, she isn't in the ballroom. If she isn't in the bathroom either... I begin to feel something I'm not accustomed to...fear. Hold on, wait, wait, wait. No. Calm down. I need to take a deep breath. I'm jumping to conclusions. Maybe she wasn't feeling well and asked Liz to take her home. But, why would she leave without telling me?

"Becca, have you seen Liz lately? Do you think she might have gone somewhere with her?" I ask, hoping no, needing the response to be yes.

"No, I left Liz in the ballroom. She's dancing with Mike." Her shaky voice tells me that my panic is spreading to her. "What's going on? Do you think something happened to Marley?"

The last thing I need right now is a frightened girl on my hands. I calm myself with my chondria's help. *Be still, peaceful, stillness, breathe, in and out.* They soothe the tension away from my muscles and regulate my breathing.

Once back under control, I realize how precarious the situation is. I need to find Marley now.

"Oh, you know what? I bet she went to use the phone in the lobby to check in with her mom," I say with a newfound air of authority. I look over Becca's shoulder. "Oh yeah, I see her."

Before Becca can turn around to see where I'm looking, I put my arm around her and lead her in the opposite direction, down a different hallway back to the ballroom.

"Don't worry about Marley, I'll look after her," I say with a big smile. "You go and have fun." I remove my arm from her shoulders and turn to head back toward the restroom.

Becca looks bewildered. "Okay, tell Marley to come and dance with us when she gets off the phone." She turns and walks back into the ballroom. I don't think Marley is going to be doing any more dancing this evening.

I walk over to the ladies' restroom door and place my hand on the doorknob. I see in my mind a lot of girls entering and leaving, but Marley has not touched it. Okay, who touched the handle about thirty minutes ago? I go through all the girls who touched the doorknob like pages in a book and come up with nothing.

Quickly I move to the front of the club and approach the front desk. "Excuse me, do you have just the one set of bathrooms down this hall?"

The older woman sitting behind the counter on a high stool glances up from her magazine. "No, we have more on the other side of the club, but they are off limits for you kids. If there's a line, you'll have to wait."

"Oh, okay," I say, smiling sheepishly.

Quickly, I walk back toward the ballroom with the woman's eyes on me. Once I'm safely in the doorway, out of sight, I watch the woman go back to her magazine. I sneak back out into the foyer and head down a dimly lit hallway toward the 'off limit' bathrooms.

There's a chair knocked over next to the ladies' room. I grasp the doorknob and again don't see Marley. But I do see Tori Lewis. There was something wrong when she touched the doorknob. If I want to find Marley, I need to find Tori.

21

FINDERS, KEEPERS

Will

I follow my instinct, leading me to the parking lot outside the country club. It's only a matter of time before I find Marley; I just hope I have enough of it. I spot Joe Reinhart's truck in the parking lot. Surely they must be nearby. As I approach the truck, I notice the driver's side door is ajar, and there is a small pool of blood on the ground next to it. I touch the door handle to find that Joe has taken a blow to the head and was dragged away by one of my kind, but it's not Malcolm. He seems familiar... I turn and follow the lead to an empty building across the road. It's a warehouse of some kind. I sense them huddled in a corner in the back.

"Joe? Tori? Are you guys in here?" I yell.

Tori calls out urgently, "Yeah, back here! Help!"

I sprint in the direction of her voice and find both Tori and Joe, back to back on the floor, tied up. Joe is barely conscious and probably has a concussion from the wound on the back of his head. Tori looks scared.

"Hold on, you guys, let me get those ropes off." When my hand touches the rope, I get an image of the same host from Joe's truck. Why can't I figure out who it is?

Once they are free, Tori puts her arms around Joe and cries, "I thought they were going to kill you, babe."

Joe will be all right after a trip to the ER. I reach into my pocket and pull out my cell. I have two calls to make. First, I call 911 and ask for an ambulance. Before I can make the second call, I need some information from these two.

"Tori, what can you tell me about who did this?"

Tori lets go of Joe and stands to face me. Tears are running down her cheeks, creating giant smudges under her eyes. She reminds me of a football player, which would be humorous under different circumstances.

"I'm sorry...he said he would hurt him...I couldn't..." Tori is shaking terribly, swiping at tears, not able to put words together.

"Tori, listen to me. I need you to tell me what happened."

"I don't know...I didn't want anything to happen to her, honest."

I place my hands on her arms, trying not to shake the answers out of her. "Tori, I know you're talking about Marley, but can you please tell me something, anything, about the person who asked you to do this?" And then it happens. The physical contact verifies who's behind this. Marley is in danger, serious danger.

"Two men. One had black hair. He just stood there and let the other one..." She starts sobbing again.

"Tori, I know. What about the other one?" I ask, forcing her to look me in the eye. I really need to know who the other one is.

She nods and looks off distantly, somehow haunted by him. "He wasn't normal. His eyes...they were so...wrong...a purplish glow. He smelled so awful, Will. I mean really bad. The one man spoke to him, but he never said anything back. He kept..." She stops and puts her head in her hands.

"He what, Tori?" I ask, forcing her head back up.

"He kept sniffing the air like an animal. Then the man told me to take the scary one into the girls' bathroom on the other side of the club. Then...oh, I'm so sorry. I really didn't want to do it, but I had to. You understand, don't you?"

"I understand, Tori. What happened next?"

"I was supposed to get Marley inside the bathroom and not let her out. I told the man it wouldn't work, but he kept threatening to hurt Joe. So I did what he said," she says, looking down at her hands.

Give me something, anything! "One last question. Did the man who spoke ever mention the other man's name?"

"Um, no...no, I don't think so."

I sigh. Why can't I place him? No matter, I know what to do next and time is of the essence. I have the lead I need, and now it's time for the second phone call.

Marley

Breathe. Now, keep breathing. I've got stay calm. Will is coming for me. He's a tracker. Even without his stone, he'll find me. It's only a matter of time. Still lying in the back of the van, I rock my body, roll onto my other side, and bite down on the cloth gag to block out the pain in my shoulders as I rotate.

I can't get the image of the boy from the bathroom out of

my head. His eyes, their hazy purple glow, the way he smelled the air, not saying a word. Something is very wrong with him. He smelled awful, as if he hadn't bathed in weeks. The hair on my neck is up as I realize his scent is all over this van.

As soon as the back door opens, hands reach for me. I struggle, trying to squirm away from them, but they grasp my shoulders and pull me out with seemingly no strain whatsoever. Unconsciously, my first thought is that my arms feel better. Quickly, I'm put down on my feet. Weakened, I immediately fall forward on my knees into the gravel. I cry out in pain as the tiny little stones bite into the skin on my knees and shins through my dress. Someone lifts me back up, leaning me against the bumper of the van. There's a bright light shining in my eyes. The urge to shield my face is overwhelming, but my hands are tied behind my back. I squint, as my eyes adjust from complete darkness to light. Finally, I'm able to make out the person standing in front of me.

Oh my God. I recognize him immediately. It's the creep from the coffee shop. His eyes are glowing like Will's, except his chondria are not green, but purple. His straight, long dark hair is slicked back into a ponytail. He's wearing a tan suit with an unbuttoned white shirt revealing a thin gold chain with some type of stone, set against a hairy chest.

With an air of arrogance, the man looks me up and down as if I'm a commodity, obviously contemplating what to do with me next. "Nice to see you again, Miss Hunter. May I untie the rope at your ankles so you can walk or should I have my boy carry you?" He nods to his right with his arm outstretched.

I follow his direction to find the scary boy from the bathroom. His purplish eyes still glow eerily. My eyes widen as my heart pounds so loudly I can hear it in my ears. I inch away from him, still leaning on the bumper, tears starting to pool in my eyes. *Keep him away from me!*

The man in front of me reaches up and pulls the gag out of my mouth, allowing it to hang around my neck. "Are you frightened of my razer?" he asks, mocking my fear.

"Y...yes," is all I can manage to squeak out of my dry throat. He's a razer! One of those hosts Will told me about, bonded against their will.

"All right then, can I untie your ankles?" he asks again impatiently.

"Uh-huh," I say, never taking my eyes off the razer, afraid that he will leap at me at any moment. There's something familiar about him too...something I can't put my finger on. Well, there's no way I want him to touch me again, ever!

As the man kneels down to untie the rope, I think about kicking him, but based on how he lifted me like a sack of potatoes from the van, he's unbelievably strong. Besides, the razer would certainly grab me before I got far, not to mention I don't know where I am or how far I could get still bound. I stand as still as I can, fighting back tears that keep slipping down my cheeks as he unties my ankles.

I look out beyond the bright light, trying to grasp at any hope of getting out of this. Where am I? It's densely wooded, with a high incline of rocks straight ahead. We must still be close to Pine Grove since we drove for about thirty minutes after I came to, and I couldn't have been out that long. I hear running water somewhere in the distance to my right. It's a trickling, a stream. It's entirely possible that it's the stream at Tumbling Run...and this might be the last time I see my woods...be near them. I turn my head the other way toward a giant house made of tan stone or stucco. There are three stories, and it seems like a football field wide. I know there are some big places up in the mountains, but this place...nothing like this. A wave of nausea makes me gag as I consider that I might die inside this house tonight. Die. Never see Mom and Ray again. Never go to school again. Never see Liz, Becca, or Anna again. Die. Never see Will...

Breathe, Marley. Breathe. I'm paralyzed, not wanting to move. What if Will doesn't find me?

The man, finished untying me, stands back to his intimidating full height. "All right, Miss Hunter." He extends his arm toward the house. "After you."

"How...do you know my name...and what do you want?" My voice cracks with fear.

He seems to evaluate me, considering answering my question, but instead, he thinks, "*All in good time, Miss Hunter, all in good time.*"

I nod and start walking slowly in the direction he indicates. My legs are barely working, but somehow I manage to stay on my feet. Desperate to try anything, I send out as much of a mental message as I can, knowing that I have no chondria to help me. I hope my connection with Will is somehow strong enough, and he will hear me.

Please, Will, I'm so scared, find me.

I stumble into the house through the front door and hear classical music playing from somewhere above. I recognize it immediately. Ray's constant classical music torments ingrained in my brain. "Air in G minor," I whisper.

The man pauses and looks at me, a smile playing at his lips. "You know classical music. Interesting," he says in a slow, creepy, yet delighted voice. Again, he seems to want to say more but thinks better of it.

The house is very well furnished and reminds me of the country club where all of my friends are still probably dancing and laughing. That is, unless my sense of time is completely off and the prom is over. We move through the foyer, passing a staircase, and continue down a narrow hallway. Old colonial pictures of people from long ago hang on the wall. I'm led to a room with mahogany double doors. The razer opens the doors and grasps me by the shoulders, shoving me inside.

"Don't you touch me!"

When I glance at the boy's eyes, he's still listless, but there's a tiny spark of recognition. He looks almost normal for a second. The man instructs me to stay in the room, and the razer shuts and locks the doors as they leave.

I whirl around. My gaze darts back and forth, taking in books lining the walls, and small pieces of furniture on the sides of the room. There are three large windows that look out the side of the house. In the center of the room is a large oak desk with a sofa placed in front of it. How long do I have? My hands are still tied behind my back, and my arms are getting more tired and sore by the minute, the reprieve from lying down to standing is over. Thankfully my ankles are free, and the gag is out. I look down at my dress and realize it's torn in a few places, and the bottom, having dragged on the ground, is filthy.

I stagger over to the windows. I can't open them without my hands, so I lean my head against the window to peer out into the darkness. Maybe there's someone hiking tonight? Yeah right, like that's even a remote possibility. I can make out lots of pine trees. This side of the house is directly alongside the forest. There isn't much else. I take one last look before I turn to face the room again. Nothing out there is going to help me.

Slowly, I move around, looking for something that might be useful. Is there a clock?

No clock.

Phone on the desk?

Nope. No surprise there. Why didn't I grab my purse with my cell phone when I went to the ladies' room? Isn't that what all girls do? I sigh. It wouldn't matter. They would have taken it from me anyway. I move over to the sofa and sit. There's nothing here to help me.

Okay, so what am I going to do? My only hope is Will. He's the only person who can help me. Where is he? Does he even know something happened to me? I try to take a deep breath, but the very large lump in my throat is making it difficult. I don't want to die. *Please God, don't let me die here.*

My voice of self-preservation says, "*Stall.*"

"Stall," I say out loud. Okay, I think I can do that. Don't let him take me anywhere, and keep him talking. I swallow the lump and wipe some fresh tears on my bare shoulder. He'll find me. I know he will. I have to keep it together. I close my eyes and take a few deep breaths. If I start to panic again, I'll crumble and not be able to go on. Will is coming for me right now. I have to believe that.

22

A PLAN

Will

Jeff is on his way to my location. I'm in the woods across from the stucco mansion. Inside are the love of my life and my worst enemy. I'm going to need Jeff's help if I have any hope to get Marley back. I can sense through the trees that the van that transported Marley has been turned off for the better part of an hour. She has to be okay. She just has to.

I was foolish not to heed Parker's warning in the parking lot and too arrogant to think that anyone could get close without my knowledge. I knew the risks of Malcolm finding out about Marley, but I had to have her, didn't I? I could have left her alone, but no, I had to mark her and make her a target for Malcolm. Who am I kidding? One of my kind would have found her eventually.

Malcolm must have slipped by my detection when I lost track of everything on the dance floor with Marley. I saw him as soon as I touched Tori Lewis's arm. He took Marley. My disadvantage is that Malcolm is unbelievably strong, and I have no plan of attack except to offer him what he wants even more than an addition to his family.

Malcolm is going to continue to make razers to spite us, and push us to tell him the location of the meteorite. But he's gone too far this time; Marley isn't someone I'm willing to bargain with. I wonder if even now, my mom is seeing all of this unfold. I haven't spoken to her since the day we honed in on Marley on the trail. If she only knew that her family needs her. She would be the one person Malcolm would listen to, since they share a close line of chondria.

"Mom, if you can hear me, I need your help. Malcolm Durst has taken Marley. I won't be able to reason with him. Please come."

On my way here, sensing Marley's fear the entire time, I called my dad. I asked him to talk to and, in a sense, take care of Joe and Tori. The last thing we need right now is those two talking to the authorities about what transpired. My dad can persuade them not to. I brought Anna with me but asked her to wait in my car parked down the road. We may need her skills, but hopefully, it won't come to that. I don't want Marley to be frightened, but if Malcolm is planning what I think he is... Well, I won't have much time to remove his chondria from her system before the bonding is complete, maybe an hour. We have only successfully saved one potential host in that manner. To this day, I'm not entirely sure the process worked.

Damn it! Where the hell is Jeff? I shake my head. Screw it. I can't wait any longer. I start moving in by myself when I hear a rustling behind me. I turn and crouch in an attack position. Sure enough, Jeff Rushmore comes creeping in behind me.

"Where the hell have you been?" I whisper sternly. "Malcolm has Marley in there. You have no idea what he could be doing to her right now! I could kill you!" I feel a distinct urgency and anger rising inside me as my chondria bounce around my insides like ping pong balls. I'm so distraught and afraid of losing Marley that I have no regret about threatening him. I can't lose her. Not now. Not after so many years of waiting...hold on...years? My emotions aren't mine anymore. My chondria. It's like *they* can't lose her or something. I shake my head, trying to clear my thoughts.

I grip the front of Jeff's shirt and lean in, so our eyes are inches from each other. "You have to help us. *We*...I mean *I*... can't lose her."

Jeff grabs my forearms and pulls my hands away from his shirt. "What's going on here? Why are you acting so emotional about this? You do this all the time. And who is *we*?" He looks away and then back, shaking his head. "You're losing it, Will. You're talking about your chondria, aren't you?"

I'm so overwhelmed, I can't respond. It feels like they're trying to take over my mind or something. What's happening? They've never acted this way with any other potential host before.

Jeff grabs me by the shoulders, his face directly in mine, eyes ablaze. "We'll get her back, but you need to get a hold of yourself. If I don't have you with me, level-headed, we may all get hurt. So snap out of it!"

I pull away and gather my thoughts. He's right. This is my body. I've got to get control of my emotions. I take a few deep breaths to steady myself. Inwardly, I yell at my chondria, "*Knock it off! This isn't helping her!*" Slowly, they ease up, allowing me to think more clearly.

I turn to face Jeff. "I'm all right."

"Really?"

"Yeah, and I've got a plan."

Marley

I've been sitting on the couch for what seems like days according to my aching arms when the tall, dark-haired man comes back into the room. I can't help myself. I'm in so much pain from the ropes around my wrists that I blurt out rather quickly, "Please untie my hands. My arms are killing me."

The man looks annoyed at my request. "Well, we can't have that, can we?" His voice drips with ice. He walks over, sits down beside me, and begins to untie my wrists. He smells of cologne and something else, something he's been cooking or eating.

"What's that smell? It smells like meat or something," I say with trepidation. Oh my God, now I have visions of Hannibal Lector in my head. Is he planning on eating...? I'm going to be sick.

He opens his mouth to respond but seems to notice my rapid breathing and pauses instead, to study me. After what seems like an eternity, he smiles cruelly and thinks, "*Don't worry, you aren't for dinner.*" He continues his thought as he loosens the final knot, freeing my hands, "*I have already eaten. It was roast pork if you're curious.*"

Oh, thank God. I have to stop watching so many movies; my life is scary enough at the moment. I can barely move my arms back to their right places by my sides because they are so sore. I moan in pain as I force myself to rotate my shoulders forward.

The man stands, towering over me, waiting for my attention. He clearly wants to have a conversation. I remind myself to take my time. I rub each of my shoulders in turn. When it's clear that I need to give him my attention, I look up. His eyes are crystal blue with shimmers of purple light illuminating his irises. He's definitely a host; of that much I'm certain. I wondered what purple would look like. The hair on the back of my neck stands up as I begin to work out a hypothesis about why I've been brought here, and it isn't a pleasant thought.

Once he knows he has my attention, he asks, "So, Miss Hunter, may I call you Marley?"

I sit there motionless, considering him. Oh, he's waiting for an answer. I cut my eyes into tiny slits, and spit back evenly, with as much confidence as I can muster, "No, you may not." I pause, waiting to see his response, which indicates a little surprise. "I remember you from the coffee shop, and you've been following me."

He smiles. "Well, I confess to a few occasions. However, I've been mostly under the radar. My daughter's been helping me."

"Look, I don't know what you think you're doing kidnapping me and bringing me here, but I assure you there are people looking for me right now." I hope my voice doesn't sound as shaky to him as it feels to me. I tell myself to be brave. "If you know what's good for you, you'll release me right now. I don't think you know who you're dealing with."

"Well, now. You have fire. I can see that," he says, clearly pleased with my performance. "Splendid. Now, please allow me to formally introduce myself. I am Malcolm Durst. Perhaps William has told you of my family. Do you know why you are here, child?"

"I'm not entirely sure, but I would appreciate it if you stopped referring to me as a child. I'm grown, or can you not tell?"

Malcolm sneers sarcastically. "Oh dear, I'm afraid I might have to call my servant in here to help you calm down. Would you like me to do that?"

"No!" I never want to see that boy again. "I'm...I'm all right. I'll be calm. Look, I think that maybe you made some kind of mistake. I don't think that you took the right person—"

"No, no, Marley. Lying doesn't become you. I must say...I expected more from William Reed's latest girl. When I think about it, you're definitely the weirdest girl I've ever seen him with." He shakes his head while making a tsk-tsk sound.

Latest girl? Me? Weird? Kettle, meet black, mister. "You're wrong, sir. I'm most certainly not Will's 'latest girl' as you put it. As a matter of fact, he should be here any minute. Then you'll be sorry." I want him to know that I'm not buying his cheap attempt to turn me against Will.

"Oh, Marley, how can you be so naïve? Honestly, did he tell you nothing? He's only courting you because you're a potential host. How can you not see that? His plan is always the same, get them bonded and leave them. Perhaps, my daughter might persuade you. Just a moment..." He looks toward the door but doesn't move. He must be communicating with another host.

The door opens, and the most beautiful girl I have ever

seen in my life walks into the room. Her hair is the color of wheat, shiny, wavy, and so long. It must be to her waist at least! She's the same height as me, but much thinner. She definitely has a supermodel's body, wearing a deep blue tank cocktail dress with matching four-inch heels. Her most striking feature is her eyes. They are huge and look like swimming pools of blue with brilliant purple flecks of light. If ever I were reminded of an angel, it would be this creature.

"Why does she always look like she's just rolled out of bed?" she says to Malcolm, rolling her beautiful eyes, clearly disapproving of me. Okay, maybe less like an angel and more like a harpy.

"Oh, Lilah, is that any way to talk to William Reed's latest catch? Please let me introduce you." He extends his arm toward me. "Lilah Durst, this is Marley Hunter." Then he turns to me. "Marley, this is my daughter Lilah. She's quite beautiful, isn't she?"

He's pleased with himself. "Yeah, just great. Listen, if it's all the same to you, why don't we call Will and have him head over here so we can straighten this out?" I'm being both sarcastic and hopeful.

Lilah laughs. It's a mean laugh. The kind of laugh you hear at school when someone falls and their books go flying. She looks at me, and says with enough venom to kill a horse, "Father, she's not only fat, but she's stupid too." She shakes her head disapprovingly again. "William is really scraping the bottom of the barrel now."

My body stills as I feel the overwhelming sense that I've heard her voice before. Then I realize where. It was her voice I heard in the bathroom at the restaurant! It was probably her who pushed me in the dress shop too! An intense, uncontrollable burning starts in my chest and works its way up to my face. Hot, white anger. What a bitch!

I leap at her. There's no way I'm going to let her get away with this. Chondria or not in those beautiful eyes, I'm going to tear each orb out one at a time. I'm caught by Malcolm before I can even get in arm's reach of Lilah. He overpowers me with one arm. My God, he's strong.

I begin clawing at his arms with all my strength, trying to escape. "Screw you, you slut! I know it was you in the bathroom and the dress shop! What's the matter? You can't face me without Daddy holding me back? You're not worth the chondria you host! You're trash!" And some other things, the heat of the moment and all that.

Lilah rolls her eyes, shifting her weight from one foot to the other impatiently. "Father, I don't have time for this. Let's get this over with."

Malcolm tightens his grip on me, and I can't breathe unless I stop fighting. I have no choice but to acquiesce.

"Listen, Marley, Will found me like all the other girls. We've all looked into those deep dark eyes and saw a future with him. He's quite the kisser, isn't he? But, that wasn't all we did..."

She stares into my face like I'm not real, only background. Then, her eyes lock onto mine. "I'll bet he started hooking up with you in shared dreams, taking you to that special island in the South Pacific? How unoriginal! I've been there with him tons of times. So if you think you're special, think again." She looks at her father for a moment with her eyebrows raised, and he nods. She turns toward the door and over her shoulder she says icily, "Nice meeting you, Marley. I look forward to my cup of tea later." Then she's gone.

I can't help but ask, "I thought you were her father? Didn't you bond her?"

"Yes, of course I did. Not all trackers bond the potential hosts they find. They simply find them. Did you think Will would be the host to bond you? That's highly unlikely, I think," Malcolm responds, clearly annoyed with how little I apparently know.

I look away, squeezing my eyes shut as he finally releases me.

I want to scream! Malcolm and Lilah are a reminder that I'm here because of Will, and he played me by taking me to his 'special island!' It's hardly special if he took that bitch there! And, what did she mean by '*that wasn't all we did*?' I'm really angry. This time, I'm not only pissed at these fools but at Will too! Why didn't I see it before? I was so taken in by his super-naturalness that I didn't realize he's like all other guys, 'latest girl,' indeed. Not to mention that this horrible girl invited me to tea later. No...wait, she said she would look forward to a cup of tea. What does that even mean?

"Oh, dear, did she upset you?" Malcolm asks innocently. "I didn't mean for her to, my child. You should take it as a compliment that one of the Reed clan has taken a shining to you. It isn't every day that William would make himself so vulnerable by sticking around for so long. He's been parading you around this small town for quite a while now. His feelings for you must be genuine. It's just that he has had so many other conquests in his rather lengthy life. It's what he does, my dear. He is and always will be a tracker. That means he'll be close with many girls like you." He sneers at me, enjoying my agony.

I explode inside. I can't take any more of this. "I'm done! I don't want to hear any more!" I yell back at him, blinking back tears. It's too much to handle. Too many emotions at once. I'm pissed, I'm sad, I'm embarrassed, I'm so stupid, and the worst part...I'm naïve.

"Yes, yes, I quite agree. Enough of that business," he says with a note of finality. "We should discuss what your role is in all of this. I know you're a potential host." He pauses, letting me absorb every word he's said.

I say nothing, but a lump forms in the back of my throat. Great, I basically just asked him to get to the point! Good one, Marley! I'm supposed to be stalling him. I continue to look him in the eye, but it's getting increasingly more difficult.

"I'll bet you know that, as well. What other reason would Will have to be so interested in a girl like you?" he asks, while his eyes trail up and down my form.

Gulp. I follow his eyes as well, looking down. My dress is a complete mess. My hair is a mess too, straggling pieces on my neck and face. The worst part is I know where his line of thinking is leading, and I don't have much time. I see the plan all laid out before me. Malcolm is going to bond me himself. It's a win-win situation for him. He will either gain a loyal family member or...or, I can barely bring myself to even think it. It's more likely I will end up as the second type of host, a razer.

"Other than your intense gray eyes, I find you to be ordinary, to say the least, but who am I to judge any vessel that can support chondria? Yes, I think you will do fine as a host."

Adrenaline rushes through my limbs again, and for the first time, I encourage it. Like lightning, I run behind the desk, a fire igniting in my heart. *Don't you dare underestimate me, you son-of-a-bitch.* Now there are two pieces of furniture between us. I scan the room for something I can use as a weapon. There's no way I'm going down without a fight.

"Don't you touch me, you disgusting excuse for a man! You don't deserve chondria!" I yell with everything I have left.

Malcolm slowly walks around the side of the couch toward me. "Now, now, Marley. Didn't Will tell you about the bonding experience? Not everyone finds it to be painful. You might be one of the lucky ones. I really don't care how you decide to host, but if you remember my servant from earlier… you might want to calm yourself and welcome the idea of being a member of my family," he says, mocking me.

Then I make the connection. I remember why his servant host looked so familiar. I saw him on television weeks ago. He's the missing boy from Texas! Think, what's his name? Sam…something. Oh my God, his poor family. They will be heartbroken when they learn about what's happened to him. Wait a minute, they'll probably never know. If I don't do something, it will be the same for my parents and me. I take a deep breath, trying to control my intense terror and panic.

"Why are you doing this?" I ask, holding on to my last bit of sanity.

He stops moving toward me. "I've been watching you and William for quite a while now. He does not typically spend this much time with a potential host. I think he believes you must be a tracker like him. He plans to train you himself. In any case, I think he cares enough about you to show up to save you. Don't you see? You're simply bait. Sure, I'll bond you, but not before I have a chance to trade you for what I really want. I think you're my best chance at finding the location of the secret meteorite, the birthplace of chondria on Earth." Malcolm raises his eyebrows, the slightest glimmer of hope in his eyes. "Perhaps you could end this entire ordeal on your own if he's already told you the location?"

So that's his game? Really? "You've got to be kidding me. I don't know where that thing is," I say, feeling helpless. "Sure, Will told me about it, but he never told me where it is, and he certainly never took me to see it." I'm going to be turned into a razer for information I don't even know!

Malcolm sighs, obviously disappointed. Then he moves toward me again. I round the other side of the desk. I'm still maintaining some distance between us. "Come now, girl, it would seem that you are going to be part of my family. In truth, I had intended to bond you regardless of Will's decision to tell me where the meteorite is." He licks his lips in anticipation of what's to come.

I can't think about that now. I need to stall this. I look directly at him, while I continue moving away, around the other side of the desk. "So that's what you do then? You take innocent potential hosts and make them your servants? Is that what you did to Sam out there?" I point toward the door. I know I'm taking a risk in goading him, but if it gives me more time, it might be what saves me. Besides, he's slowly gaining ground on me as we do our dance around the desk and couch.

"Oh, I see. You know my servant from his picture on the news. His parents looked so sad, didn't they?" He's oozing cynicism and false concern.

Okay, now what? I need to do something. I'm scanning the room again when I hear Will.

"Marley, I'm here. I'm coming for you. Hold on," Will thinks to me as clearly as if he were in the room with us. My heart skips a beat.

He's here.

All my pent up anger toward Will melts away, and I know I have to survive so I can touch him and look into his eyes one more time. I regain some courage.

But it's short lived when I hear a different voice in my head.

"I know he's here too. What will he choose? You or the location of the meteorite? It's time to find out. We can do this willing or unwilling, but I warn you, chondria will know your thoughts and desires. You need to make a choice. I assume Will told you about the two methods for bonding. I would never force myself upon you so put that out of your mind. It will be a blood bond for us," Malcolm thinks calmly with a note of finality.

Wait, what is he talking about? Two ways to bond? Is he referring to sex? The thought turns my stomach. He pulls out a syringe from the interior of his jacket, rolls up his sleeve, and draws blood from his arm. Are you kidding me? I'm going to be sick. It's so dark and thick flooding out of his arm into the vial. The room moves around me. It dawns on me why Will never told me about the bonding process. He knew how I would feel...nausea and lightheadedness takes over. The room spins.

I reach out for something to grab onto, but everything is black.

23

AN APOLOGY

Will

"**C**ome on, Jeff, hurry up! Give me the damn signal!" I think
as loudly as I possibly can to Agent Rushmore.

From outside the window, I see Malcolm drawing blood
from his arm in front of her. She sways, her eyes fluttering.
Marley is terrified of needles and the sight of blood; something very serious considering how most hosts bond with
chondria. Oh no, she's going down!

Just then there's a loud crash outside the library door. The
signal! Jeff must be working his way into the room. It's now or
never, and I can see Malcolm looking toward the door. I kick
the window, shattering the glass, and scramble inside. My
instinct is to go to Marley, but I go after Malcolm first. I tackle
him as he turns to see the broken window. We fall to the
ground, me on top of him, and the syringe goes flying across
the floor. We roll around, trading kicks and punches. I'm on
the receiving end of most of them. This is going to be a losing
battle if Jeff doesn't get in here now.

Malcolm grabs me by the back of the neck and sneers in my face, "Give me the location of the meteorite, and I'll leave her alone."

"I'll die before I let that happen," I say, biting back the pain Malcolm is now placing on my neck. He could snap me like a twig anytime he wants to, but we both know he needs me. This is a mission of pain only, and I have to endure it for Marley's sake.

Then Jeff Rushmore comes through the door of the library wielding a Glock pistol aimed directly at Malcolm and me. Malcolm has the advantage, though, as he has me by the neck, shielding his body behind mine.

"I will break his neck if you don't put that gun down, Agent Rushmore," Malcolm states, playing his game.

"Jeff, don't do it! Save Marley!" I yell, trying to turn my head to look for her.

Marley

I regain consciousness and realize all hell is breaking loose around me. My head is still floating, but I see Will fighting with Malcolm. I know how strong Malcolm is, and that means Will is in serious trouble. Agent Rushmore is here, wearing his usual black suit but no sunglasses this time. He has a gun in his hand and looks ready to use it. Good.

When I look back toward Will and Malcolm, I realize it's too late. Malcolm has Will by the throat, and he's going to kill him! Kill him! No! I can't let this happen. I have to do something. Desperately, I look around on the floor for a weapon, only finding the syringe Malcolm used to draw his blood. Gross! I grab it, trying not to think about its contents, and crawl over to the desk. There, underneath the right side, I find a kitchen knife. How did that...

Before I finish the thought, Anna's voice is thundering in my head. "*Sorry, it's all I could find! Use it if you have to, Marley.*"

I swallow hard and pick it up. Malcolm's attention is on Agent Rushmore. I palm the handle of the knife, concealing it up my left forearm, and grasp the syringe in my right hand. Slowly, I stand.

"Hey, Malcolm, let him go," I say, my tone serious, gaining confidence as the cool metal of the knife tickles at the fleshy part of the back of my arm. I have to get him to let Will go. As calmly as I can, I plead, "Please, you don't need him...you have me. Obviously, he isn't going to tell you where the meteorite is but you can still have me." I hold out the syringe. "That's what you want anyway, isn't it?"

Malcolm looks thoughtful and whispers something to Will. Then, to me, he says, "Miss Hunter, you surprise me with your bravery. But as you see, I'm in a bit of a precarious situation with a gun pointed at me. You'll have to inject yourself to prove you mean it." He smiles maliciously.

Well, hell! That's not part of my plan! I'm not very good at this sort of thing! How does a person prepare for dangerous situations in which her boyfriend is about to be killed, and she might be turned into a mindless human host? I have no clue, and I'm obviously terrible at it. Luckily, Agent Rushmore comes to my rescue.

"Malcolm, look, I'll put down my gun if you let him go? All right?" Jeff says, holding out both his hands in surrender.

"No, Marley, don't do this. Jeff, please don't put your gun down!" Will yells.

I'm not entirely sure, but I think Anna told both Will and Jeff about the knife. I can't believe Jeff's confidence in me. But here we are. Slowly Jeff bends over, laying his gun down on the floor and stands back up.

"Kick it over to me," Malcolm says.

Jeff acquiesces, sliding the gun with amazing precision to Malcolm's foot. Malcolm bends down and grasps the gun. He throws Will down on the ground and kicks him in the stomach.

"No! Stop! Please, don't!" I yell, not wanting Will to endure any more pain.

Malcolm tucks the gun in the back of his pants and wastes no time striding over to me. He takes the syringe out of my hand and grasps my right arm.

I take one last look at Will, and our eyes meet. In my head, I hear, "*I love you.*"

So many images flash through my mind—Will in the nurse's office wearing his signature t-shirt and jacket, the trails when he first asked me to the prom, his firefly eyes in my dreams, Tumbling Run where he first told me about his true identity, Tamarind for our first date, walking in the park, our first kiss, watching him track on a warm afternoon, dancing at the prom... the people I care about... Becca, Justin, Liz, Anna, Ray, my mom...Will. The last image I have is of a sad deer lying on the ground. A man wearing camouflage and orange uses a knife to split the deer's belly open. I turn away, but it's too late. I've already seen the deer's slippery organs spill out onto the grass.

"*I love you too,*" I think, even though I know he can't hear me. A single tear slips down my cheek as I turn my attention back to Malcolm. He's poised to put the syringe in my arm. I grip the handle of the knife, turning it in my left hand and take a step back. Malcolm senses my movement, but it's too late. I press forward with all my weight, plunging the knife into his chest with all my strength.

Malcolm drops the syringe and grasps me by the shoulders, in shock. He's gripping me so tightly I do the only thing I can think of to make him stop. I lean even closer, pushing the edge of the knife deeper into his chest, somehow sensing the tip pierce his heart. The voice inside my head whispers, "*I'm sorry.*"

His eyes bulge, chondria swirling in recognition as he falls to the floor.

I look down at my hand. It's covered in warm red slick, and it's sticky between my fingers. Something metallic is in the air. *Oh. Oh no, what did I do?* The last thing I hear before I pass out again is Will's voice yelling for Anna.

* * *

I'M DREAMING. It's my dream, not shared with a host. I know this because my dad's here and no host could ever have known him.

We're standing on a beach with the waves lapping at our feet as they sink deeper into the sand. I look up at him and know in my heart that he loves me.

"Dad, I did something terrible. I think I killed someone. I didn't want to, but I didn't have a choice. What should I do?"

He looks at me as if seeing me for the first time. Slowly, he replies, "Look at the waves swirling around your feet, Marley. What do you see?"

I look down at the sea stroking my legs back and forth. It's rhythmic and soothing. It isn't a dark blue as I thought it should be. It's blue-green with fluorescent lights floating under the surface.

"Chondria?"

"Yes, Marley, chondria. They have already forgiven you. He'll help you understand," he says, putting his arm around my shoulders.

"You mean Will," I say, more as a statement than a question.

"Yes. I'm so proud of you. You've grown into such a beautiful young woman. Please tell your mother I loved her, and I love you. I'll see you again."

Then, before I can say anything else, he moves out into the water, diving into the waves until finally he's gone.

How is this possible? Should I follow him, and swim out into the ocean? I don't think I can. Everything inside me is pulling me back toward the shore. Then I hear Will's voice calling for me.

"Will? I hear you. Where are you?" I shout into the void.

I glance back down, as chondria swirl round and round in a circular pattern around my feet. It's mesmerizing.

A voice rises to the surface in my mind, like many voices speaking in unison, "*Marley, all is not as it seems. I am real, like you. Don't let him forget. You are the key to my voice.*"

24

JANE REED

Will

I can't believe she did it. *Oh my God! I think Marley killed Malcolm Durst!*

"Anna! Get in here!" I yell, knowing my mom and sister are right behind Jeff.

Anna rushes into the grim scene. Marley is on the floor passed out next to Malcolm, whose still-open eyes tell me he's no longer alive. I check his pulse just in case. Nothing. His chondria will die if we don't move quickly. Anna understands immediately and raises her hands, chondria illuminating her fingertips. The knife flies out of his chest and clatters on the floor. Gradually, as if Malcolm's skin is translucent, purple chondria glow throughout his body. Then they move, traveling toward his chest, and the site of his wound.

"Okay, Will, where am I going with them? I can take some."

"No. None of us is taking any of them," my mom says sternly, from behind Anna.

"What are you talking about, Mom? We can't let them die," I say, leaning down next to Marley.

"That's not what I said. I don't want any of us to take his chondria. Malcolm wasn't right, and we have no way of knowing if his chondria were affected. The only safe thing to do is put them in him," she says, pulling Sam Wyatt into the room.

Poor Sam, as if he hasn't endured enough already. But... she's right, of course. He already has Malcolm's chondria in his body. It won't hurt him or make things any worse than they already are. "Okay, I agree, but we have to get Sam to Dr. Arcanas as soon as possible." Then I look at Anna, simply nodding.

I pull Marley, who is still unconscious, into my arms, while my mom leads Sam over to Malcolm's body. She picks up the knife and makes a small cut on his palm. He doesn't even flinch. What have the Dursts been doing to this poor kid? They kneel down next to Malcolm as my mom presses Sam's hand over the wound. Anna uses her ability to push chondria into Sam's hand. Their brightness flows into Sam and up his arm. After a minute, Anna puts down her hands. The transfer is complete. Malcolm is dead, but his chondria are safely in one of his razers. Oddly appropriate.

"Mom, why isn't she waking up?" I ask, barely able to contain my emotions about the girl lying in my arms, who I love so much. There's nothing I can do. I hate feeling this helpless. I want to punch something really hard. It's agonizing.

"Honey, she's exhausted. It's been a horrible ordeal for her. She just killed a man. Let her rest."

I can't explain it, but my chondria won't let it go. "Are you sure she's okay? I can't bear to..." I can't finish. I'm overwhelmed with emotion.

My mom looks confused, then thoughtful. "Are you saying you love her?"

My eyes stay focused on Marley.

My mom stands and starts pacing. Her thoughts pour out like a stream in my head, "*I should have been here to see and help you. It was bad timing, my helping our friends. William, how did this happen? How did I not see you mark the wrong girl?*"

I'm barely listening. Marley's face seems to relax as she eases into a deep sleep.

"*Rest, Marley. You'll feel better when you wake. I'll be here waiting for you,*" I say, mind to mind.

"*William! What happened?*" my mom thinks persistently.

Finally, I look up at her, and for the first time realize what she's been saying to me. It really sinks in.

"What do you mean Marley is the wrong girl? That she's not a viable host? How is that possible? I found her in the precise location that you saw in your vision," I say with defiance, and a twinge of anger at this new revelation.

My mom looks grief stricken as she puts her hands to her temples, massaging. I've seen her do this countless times when she's trying to rid herself of bad thoughts. Finally, she looks back at me. "You love her, Will. That is plain as day. This is both wonderful and tragic. I think you will feel the same way once I explain everything to you."

"There's no time for explaining. We need to get out of here and back home. Marley's parents will be wondering where she is, and I don't think I can explain her current condition. I'll have to improvise. We can talk after I make sure she's safe."

"All right, you're right," she thinks, placing her hand on my shoulder. I feel a tremor of the truth. I push down my fear of the future and a life without Marley. Instead, I pick her up, her head resting against my chest.

By the time we're on the main road back to town, Marley regains consciousness. She's groggy at first, murmuring something about chondria, and I distinctly hear her say my name. Once she's fully aware, she seems to be all right. There's no time to think about what happened and what we'll have to face, given this new information. Right now, she's wearing a dirty dress and looks exhausted. She needs rest and some kind of plan to deal with her parents.

Fortunately, I brought Marley's purse with me when I took off after her. She takes out her cell and makes two calls. The first to her friend Liz, and the second to her parents. After she hangs up, she looks overly drained, but still manages, "Done, I'm good until tomorrow morning. Now, what are we going to do about this dress?"

"You let me take care of that. You're going to stay at my house and borrow something of Anna's," I say, taking her back into my arms.

She puts her head on my chest. As she slowly starts to drift off, she says, "Okay, but I don't think any of her things will fit me." She stretches a little and murmurs, "It feels good to be in your arms..." Then she's asleep again. I touch her hair, resting my chin on her head. She's alive, she's safe, and she's the only woman I will ever love.

I have a lot to think about, and much to discuss with my mom. Now might be as good a time as any to resolve this. I already suspect what happened, and why I'm holding this girl who means everything to me, and not someone else.

"*We should talk while Marley is sleeping,*" I think to my mom.

"*I've been waiting, giving you some time to think,*" my mom thinks from the driver's seat.

I can't see her facial expression from my place in the backseat, but I sense her sadness.

"*The last time we spoke, before you left, you guided me to Marley on the trail. As soon as I saw her, I sensed that she was the one. How is it possible now that she's not a viable host?*" I'm anxious and desperate for some kind of explanation.

My mom pulls the car over to the side of the road and turns off the engine. She turns to Anna in the passenger seat. A few seconds pass and Anna gets out of the car. Finally, she twists her body around the driver's seat to face me.

"I love you, and I want you to be happy. I hope you know that. I have no doubt that as soon as you saw her; you thought she was the one for you. She just wasn't the one you were there to mark. I also know you've been searching for someone like her for a while now. That's why it happened. You wanted it to be her so badly. But, son, you were wrong."

My mom confirms what I already know and should have known all along. I was so blinded by her. She felt so right to me. The idea that I had found someone I felt such a connection to...it was too tempting. Somehow I jumped to a conclusion that I shouldn't have. I marked her before I could even think twice about it. Once it was done, I was helpless to detect anything except guidance and protection for her. I've never been wrong before. How could I be wrong now?

"Why are you saying this? I still sense that she's supposed to be one of us. If what you are saying is true, why did I mark her? Am I that terrible of a tracker? She could have been killed tonight by Malcolm." I look down at Marley in my arms.

"I know it's terribly disheartening to think about, but I assure you, it's true. She is not a potential host. If you pursue her, you will most assuredly kill her."

I know that my mom's right. It's as simple as that. If Marley isn't a potential host, she will die if I try to bond her. Still, I can't stand not having any hope. I need to ask. "Mom, are you absolutely sure she isn't a potential host? If there is any way, I need to know."

My mom's chondria light up her eyes. "I will try to see, but I can't guarantee anything." She reaches out her hand and touches Marley's arm. Her eyes close as she attempts to connect with Marley's future. Her eyebrows wrinkle and form a line across her forehead as she concentrates. A few minutes pass. Finally, she lets go and shakes her head, breathing heavily.

"It's too clouded. I can't make everything out, but I saw nothing of you. I believe it's because I'm too close to you and, therefore, her. I can't get a clear reading. I'm very sorry." A tear runs down her cheek.

I've fallen for the wrong girl. Hell, I don't care. I wouldn't change it for anything. Even if I only spend one more day with her, it will be more meaningful than the rest of my life without her. There's something about her, something she makes me feel that's essential for my existence. I breathe her in and can't imagine a life without her. I always wondered what it would be like to have a soul mate.

Unfortunately for me, now I know.

Marley

Lying in a strange bed, I wake to sunlight streaming in through the blinds of a window. I squint, trying to remember how I got here. It doesn't take long to piece it all back together—the prom, the abduction, the blood, ugh, my stomach turns at the thought of it. I think of Will, and agreeing to spend the night at their house. I pull myself up against the pillows and look around the room. It's painted lavender with a pretty lilac border. There's whitewashed bedroom furniture, and the bedspread in front of me is white with a pattern of lilacs. I must be in Anna's room. Oh, I hope she isn't sleeping on the couch because of me. I need to use the bathroom, but I don't want to get up and face the day yet. There's so much to think about.

I stretch out my arms, turning away from the window. It's time to face a few facts. First, and most importantly—I'm pretty sure I killed Malcolm Durst last night. I...killed someone. I cover my mouth, stifling a cry. A voice inside my head says, '*you had no choice.*' Is that true? Did I have a choice? No, I didn't. I saw the truth in Malcolm's eyes. It was him or me. If I hadn't done what I did, he would have turned me into a shell of a human being. Worse, he could have killed Will anyway. I could never, ever let that happen.

Will. Damn him! How could he ever date Lilah Durst? I don't really care about other girls he's dated, but her? Disgusting! Also, Malcolm said Will had '*a rather lengthy life.*' What's up with that? Has Will been lying to me about his age? I've got a feeling there's a lot more he still has to tell me, and I don't think I'm going to like any of it.

When I finally move from the bed to the mirror on the wall, I realize I need more than a quick splash of water on my face. My hair is a mess, sticky with hairspray, and my eyeliner has run down my cheeks like black waterfalls. This...this is why I don't normally wear makeup. Liz would call me a *'hot mess.'* I definitely need a shower.

I EMERGE from the bathroom feeling better. One of the Reeds left me a new toothbrush, toothpaste, soap, two little bottles of shampoo and conditioner like you get in a hotel, and a warm towel that must have been right out of the dryer. As I traverse the stairs, I remind myself to thank them for their hospitality. As soon as I step off the last step, I smell bacon and follow the scent to the kitchen. There, I find the entire Reed family moving around, putting breakfast on the table.

Will looks up at me first, coming to my side. Obviously concerned, he asks, "How are you? Did you sleep all right? We're getting some breakfast together. Are you up to eating?"

Everyone stops mid-motion to wait for my answers. It's very unnerving. My eyes fill with tears that I can't seem to stop. "Well, I guess I'm as good as can be expected for a person who just took someone's life."

"Marley..."

I swipe at the tears in my eyes and take a deep breath. "Look, I'm sorry. Forget I said that. It's just that I never in a million years would have thought that I could do something like that. It's overwhelming."

"I know. I'm so sorry you were in that position."

Then Robert is by my side, taking my arm. "Marley, I'll help you, but it's going to take some time. Don't rush it."

I instantly feel better in his charismatic, capable hands. "Thank you." I exhale the breath I was holding. Enough of this for now. Besides, there are other things on my mind. I glance back at Will. "What can I do to help?"

The only Reed I haven't met approaches me. Jane Reed is tall with dark hair like Will's, even though they aren't biologically related. She walks with an air of dignity and respect. The odd thing is she seems young, almost too young to be Will's mother. She can't be more than thirty years old. I recognize her from somewhere as well. "It's nice to finally meet you," she says, her intense green eyes aglow.

"Nice to meet you, too, Mrs. Reed," I reply, smiling shyly. Please tell me she's not reading my mind. Oh, please...

"*Don't worry, honey. I can't read minds, and please call me Jane,*" she thinks, a mirthful smile on her lips.

I laugh uncertainly. "Jane," I respond, aloud.

Will takes my hand. "I think we're all set. Let's sit down."

He leads me to a chair at the table. There are eggs, bacon, toast, and pancakes on the table. I hate to admit it, but I'm starving. Then they all take each other's hands. Will nudges me to do the same with him and Anna on my other side.

Robert looks at me. "I normally say thanks before a meal. I hope that's all right?"

"Sure," I reply.

Robert smiles. "I'm thankful for the health of my family, and that Marley may be with us for this meal."

"You don't like your given name, Marlena?" Jane asks, smiling warmly.

She knows my full name, something I seldom mention. Oh, her special gift. I look at my lap, feeling like the center of attention. "My mom loved the name, but I prefer Marley. Marlena seems so formal and long."

Anna squeezes my hand and compliments me, "It's a pretty name."

"Will feels the same way, you know, but I love the name William," Jane says looking at her son.

"*Marlena is a beautiful name*," Will says in my head.

I glance at him, smiling slightly. He looks sad or something. I open my mouth to ask what's wrong, but he looks away and shifts uncomfortably in his seat. What's that about?

After a long pause, everyone drops hands to eat. Anna puts her hand out and catches a napkin that goes sailing across the table from a holder, placing itself on her lap. She's using her special gift. I gasp as it still amazes me.

"Anna! Not at the table, think of your guest," Jane says in a reprimanding tone.

"Oh, Mom, she's seen me do plenty, and she doesn't mind. Do you, Marley?"

Jane looks from Robert to me. "I guess I've been away too long. I didn't realize how much I'd missed." She looks as though she feels guilty or something. About what, I'm not entirely sure.

"No. It's fine. Anna's gift is a fascinating thing. I think all of you are pretty great, and I'm in awe of your incredible abilities. I wonder what my special ability will be." I reach for the plate of eggs.

Everyone at the table stops mid-motion. What? What did I say? It's so quiet that I can hear the ice melting in my glass of water. Based on their expressions, it must be pretty loud in their heads.

Aloud, Robert says, "Will, now is not the time."

"Your father is right, don't..." Jane adds.

Will pushes his seat back from the table and faces me,

grasping my hands in his. His eyes are like two sheets of glass. Something is really wrong. Oh no, he hates me for what I did to Malcolm. Or maybe he knows that I know about the other girls. Either way, I don't really want to discuss this in front of his family.

"Will, we can talk about this later. Okay?" I say quietly.

"She's right, now isn't—" Jane says.

Will looks at his mom and cuts her off. "I can't. I'm not going to sit here and pretend like everything's okay. I've made a mess of this, and I can't take it anymore. For God's sake, Marley killed a man last night because of me!"

"Will—" I start, but he cuts me off too.

"Stop. Everyone just...stop." Then, blocking everyone else out, Will looks into my eyes with desperation. "I'm sorry. I can't keep pretending like this. I have to tell you the truth. I hope someday you'll find it in your heart to forgive me. I made a mistake that first time I saw you on the trail. I was so overcome...I...I wanted it to be you." A single tear cascades down his right cheek. He swipes at it and continues, "Marley, you aren't a potential host. I hope you'll someday forgive me and at least think of me as a friend."

25

ALL IS REVEALED

Marley

Not a potential host? We're going to be friends? What is this crap all about? I stand, confusion taking over. "I'm so sorry, please excuse me." I quickly walk out of the kitchen. I need to get out of here. Before I get to the hall, Will's mom is next to me, touching my arm. I look into her sad eyes as she thinks the truth to me.

"I'm so sorry, Marley. It's really my fault. I wasn't here when he marked you. Please don't be too angry with him. He loves you."

"No," is all I can manage as I remove her hand.

I'm out the front door, with bright sunlight beating down when I realize I don't have any shoes on, or my dress, or a way to get home. I look over at Becca's house longingly, but that wouldn't be a smart move, since I'm supposed to be at Liz's. I turn around to go back into Will's house when Anna appears in the doorway.

"Marley, come back inside. We can go up to my room to talk and get your dress. When you're ready to leave, I'll take you home. I promise, okay?" She's being kind, and I don't want to refuse. Still...

"I appreciate it, Anna, but I'm really confused, and I don't want to see Will," I say, hoping she won't pressure me further.

She turns around, glancing back inside the house. When she faces me again, she smiles triumphantly. "I told him to get lost. He's not in the house anymore." She's clearly not going to take 'no' for an answer.

"Anna, I..." I can't do this. I don't want to talk to her about what happened. I still need to process.

"*Come here, Marley,*" Anna thinks, eyes sad, with her arms outstretched.

Suddenly, as if my body has a mind of its own, I hug her... and I don't mind at all that she must have *pulled* me a little.

I leave a trail of dampness on her shoulder, but quickly wipe it away. "Anna, what am I going to do?"

Anna, looking wiser than her age, replies, "You're going to come upstairs with me. That's what you're going do."

I hesitate but acquiesce. "As long as *he's* not here...I do need my dress and a ride home."

Anna smiles, reassuring me, as I follow her back into the house and up to her room. Along the way she says, "Say, I hope my clothes are okay, and that you had all the stuff you needed in the bathroom. I was in charge of that."

"Thanks for everything, Anna. I'm sorry if I am being rude now. It's just that..." I can't put the rest of the words together.

But I don't have to because Anna thinks, "*Don't worry, I know, it's okay.*"

I go into her bedroom while she goes to get my dress from another room. I dread seeing the state of my beautiful prom dress after everything that happened last night. It must be trashed. Seriously, how could it not be?

But to my surprise, Anna brings in my dress, wrapped in plastic, looking as it did the day I purchased it at the store. I can't believe my eyes. "How did you...I mean...it was torn and...oh thank you, Anna." I get up to hug her again.

She has a look of confusion on her face, then recognition, as she holds out her hand to stop me. "Don't thank *me*, Marley; you should thank Will. He took care of it for you. I was in charge of shampoo, remember?" she says with a quirky smile.

"Wait, Will knows how to sew? That's so...um, not like him." I shake my head, confused.

Anna laughs. "No, of course not, but Mr. Graham does."

Wait...how did Will get Mr. Graham to sew my dress? It was the middle of the night when we got back to his house. This doesn't make any sense.

Before I can ask how it happened, Anna continues, "Will made some phone calls to a dry cleaner, and then he went over to Mr. Graham's house. He only got back home about an hour before you got up. He told Mr. Graham that he stepped on your dress and couldn't stand the thought of it being ruined. I guess Mr. Graham felt bad for him and took care of it right then and there. Isn't that sweet?"

I'm not sure if she means Will or Mr. Graham, but it was very kind of both of them. Oh crap, maybe I shouldn't have walked out during breakfast. Everyone must think I'm so rude. Will and his family clearly care about me. I swallow the lump in my throat, and all I can say is, "Yeah."

"So listen, I think you should at least hear what my brother has to say before you go home today. He and I have our fights, but he's still my brother. I have never seen him so wrecked in all the time that I've known him. Do you think you could find it in your heart to talk to him?" Her eyes are pleading his case.

I'm so confused and upset about what he said at breakfast, but I also know I should be mature about this. The conversation is going to happen sooner or later. Better to get it over with now. "I guess it's the right thing to do," I whisper to both Anna and myself.

Anna hugs me, and with her chin on my shoulder she thinks, "*He's out back.*"

Will

I sense her eyes on me before I even turn around. Maybe there's a chance she'll listen. I stand, turning to face her as the screen door clatters shut.

"Marley...I feel like such an ass. Will you hear me out?"

"You *are* an ass. Why should I talk to you? So you can give me some explanation about how we'll be great friends? How you screwed up? How we can never be together? How with time I'll find someone who's right for me? And how you will too? Well, that isn't what I want, and..." She's faltering, her eyes filling up with tears. I move toward her, the thought of her being this upset tearing me up inside. But she holds up her hand and takes a deep breath. "I really don't want to hear any of it."

I can't handle it. I have to hold her, even if she fights me; I have to be near her. My chondria are still drawn to her, still protective of her. I reach my hands around her waist and pull her to my chest. "*That isn't what I want either.*"

I come undone as she puts her arms around my neck, hugging me back. "I hate that I can't resist you," she mutters to herself.

I push her hair aside and gently kiss her left temple. She's so beautiful. It hurts to even think about being without her.

Grasping her hand, I lead her toward a wicker sofa, passing the goldfish pond. Peering down into the pond, she notices the glowing fish. She opens her mouth to ask, but I think, "*Don't, it's an experiment of my dad's.*"

She nods, a quizzical look on her face.

She sits down on the couch, and I slide into a chair opposite her. I've got some explaining to do, and I don't exactly know how she'll react. Better keep some distance.

She's pressing her hands on her thighs, trying hard not to ball them up into fists like she always does when she's nervous. I raise my eyebrows at her.

"Marley, I—"

"So I have some questions, and I want you to be totally honest with me. Can you do that? I think after everything that happened last night, I've earned it."

Okay. She's not beating around the bush. "Yeah, sure. Ask me anything." I lean forward, my forearms on my thighs.

"Are you really seventeen?" she asks quickly, probably hoping to catch me off guard.

I thought this might come up. My eyes never leave hers as I reply, "Yes...but I've been seventeen for a few years now."

Her mouth opens in surprise as she stares at me. Her mind is working in overdrive, trying to understand what I said. It reminds me of when I first told her what I was. She was shocked then too.

"How's it possible to be the same age for a *few* years?"

I smile. "Well, let me explain it to you this way. People get cosmetic surgery all the time to look younger, right?"

She nods.

"Well, I simply have the means to look younger already inside me. I started aging much slower than the average human the moment I became a host. Two things make this possible. First, my DNA combined with chondria DNA simply slows down the aging process. Also, my chondria repair and sustain my body at an exponentially faster rate than your body. This is part of the reason why we don't stay in the same place for long periods of time."

"Do you ask your chondria to do that?" she asks, seeming more curious than shocked now.

"Actually, no. I think they do it for environmental purposes."

She shakes her head, obviously confused. "Environmental purposes?"

"Okay, how about this... Do your parents decorate your house and fix things when they break?"

"Of course they do, but what does that—"

"Exactly," I say, satisfied. "That's what chondria do. They do a lot of updating because it's more comfortable to live in a place that's fresh and new. Get it?"

"Oh, so chondria like to live in style?" she asks, mocking my analogy.

No. That's not it at all. Frustrated, I try to think of another way to explain it to her.

She holds up her hand. "Don't worry, I get it, keep your shirt on."

Keep my shirt on? Oh. She's joking. Still, she's staring at

my chest. I smile seductively at her, leaning down to catch her eyes. "Okay, shirt stays on."

She ignores my comment. "Wait a second, so if you're seventeen physically, and based on what you said, doesn't that make you a lot older in your head? Are you like an old man trapped in a boy's body or something? Because *that* would be really creepy."

I can't help it; I start laughing so hard that tears come to my eyes. "Now, that...that's hilarious. I'll have to tell my family that one."

She raises her eyebrows questioningly.

"No, I'm not an old person. My chondria have kept my mind the same age as the rest of my body. I simply maintain my age for longer than you do. Everything I think and feel is like any other seventeen-year-old." How else to explain it? "Have your parents ever reminded you of what you were like when you were a kid?"

"Sure, my mom said that I was a handful when I was six. I wouldn't sit still, and I was always getting into trouble."

"Well, imagine how my mom felt when she had to deal with a two-year-old for three years." I smile mischievously.

"So then, what's your actual birth date?"

My smile is gone instantly. I don't want to talk about this. Not now at least. I sigh remembering that I promised to answer all of her questions. "The orphanage didn't actually have a birth date for me when I came to them. I was...found, alone. They guessed based on a physical, and it's November 11, 1961. My mom adopted me soon after I arrived at the orphanage," I say slowly, not able to look at her even once.

"That's why your mom looked so familiar to me. She was in a newspaper article about a meteorite found here. Mr.

Bradshaw showed it to me. She was carrying a baby. That was you, wasn't it?"

I nod. I carry a copy of that article folded up in my wallet.

Her eyes never leave me. But, I can't seem to meet them. I feel so ashamed. I have no real birthday. No idea who my birth parents are, or why they left me. I don't want her pity, not about this.

Then she's up, moving to sit on the arm of my chair. Her hand rests on my shoulder. It's startling, but her touch soothes me.

"I'm sorry, I didn't know," she says.

I put my hand on her thigh and gaze up at her. "It's fine, don't worry about me." I brush off the sadness and focus my concern back on her. "I'm more worried about you and what happened with Malcolm. How're you doing?"

She takes a deep breath and sighs. "Honestly, I've kind of been blocking it out, but I guess I can't do that forever. The thing is, I felt like I didn't have a choice. Do you know what I mean? It was like it was him or me...and I chose me."

"I know that, but still, you must have some feelings about the fact that he's dead now?" Knowing it was my fault in the first place, I add, "I hate that you were even in that position."

Marley stands, wanting to be clear. "I'm sorry he died. I really didn't want that, but like I said, I had no choice. I'm even sorrier about his chondria. I guess they all died too?"

"Actually, no, we were able to save them."

"Seriously? How?" she asks, amazed.

"Anna did it with her ability."

"Right, but where did she put them? They can't live outside of a body, can they?"

Uh-oh. She isn't going to like this. "Well, they can live

inside blood, but we didn't exactly have any on hand so..." I trail off, not able to put the words together. She is going to be pissed.

"And? Where did you put them?"

"Well...we put them in Sam Wyatt, the razer who took you from the prom," I say, bracing for her response.

As I hear her sharp intake of breath, I quickly continue, "It was a temporary fix. Jeff Rushmore took him to a host physician who will take care of him." I'm pleading, I know, but I can't stand the thought of her being afraid of Malcolm's chondria seeking vengeance on her. In all honesty, that could very well be possible.

Her expression is difficult to read. She doesn't really seem upset, just confused or something. "Okay, so, will Malcolm's chondria remember what I did?"

All right, she gets it. It's probably best to go with the truth. "We honestly don't know."

She puts her hand to her forehead. Clearly, the repercussions of what happened are sailing through her mind. Do I think that Malcolm's chondria are seeking out vengeance on her from inside Sam's body? Possibly. But I would never let him near her.

"Oh my God, Will," she says, rubbing her temples.

"Marley, don't worry about it. It's all taken care of, I promise. Let's focus on you and us. Do you have any more questions for me?" I ask, trying to change the subject.

"Okay, fine. So Malcolm told me that you've had a lot of 'potential host' girlfriends, but I guess considering what you just told me that makes sense now. Lilah said she was one of them, and I have to tell you, Will, she is *not* a nice person. I don't know what you were thinking there." She rolls her eyes.

"But something she said makes me wonder about, well, you know, if you've slept with a lot of girls..." She glances down at Anna's borrowed flip flops, flexing her toes, her cheeks getting red again.

God, no. I could never...especially not knowing what I feel now. I lift her chin, making sure our eyes meet. "No, I've not, and I never will. Please believe that because I mean it."

"Wait, what do you mean, you never will?" she asks, confused.

"I can only ever be intimate with someone who is a host or a potential host. I mean, I'm not going to lie to you; I've messed around, but never sex. That's one of the two ways to bond someone. It's universally reserved for two people who intend to share their lives together. It's how my mom bonded my dad." I pause to remember their bonding ceremony. "At least you'll know that. I promise you I'll never share that with another person. That's all I have to give you right now. I know it isn't much, but..."

"So wait, are you saying that we can never..." she begins, and then she somehow realizes the seriousness of what I'm actually saying. As things stand now, we can never be a true couple.

"So we can't be together because I'm not a potential host," she says, almost more to herself than to me. Then she looks up and meets my eyes. There's determination there. She wants to know why. "But, there's one thing I don't understand. What happened? Why did you think that I was a potential host? Please be honest with me. Why?"

Now we get to the heart of it. I'm about to break her heart into a million pieces, and I know it. But there's nothing to be done about it. I just have to say it. I owe her at least that. I take her hand in mine. "This is going to be difficult to hear, but I need you to know that I made the mistake because I wanted it to be you. Please don't hate me. I don't think I could handle that." I look into her eyes, beseeching.

"I don't know, let's hear it first," she replies honestly.

I sigh. "I understand."

Then I'm fidgeting, something I rarely do. I don't know how to say this. I glance up at her and can tell she knows it's really bad. Well, here goes.

"You remember when I first touched your shoulder in the ravine?"

"Yeah..."

"Well, when I first saw you, I wanted you to be the potential host. Then, I felt my chondria pull me toward you on the trail, and Marley, my chondria have never been wrong. So, I had no reason to believe it wasn't you. I marked you without even thinking twice about it."

She looks around, processing what I've said. Please don't make me say it outright. My skin crawls with the pain of what she is about to understand. Her mind is working, her eyes darting back and forth, trying to figure it out. Shock transforms her face as she works out the truth. She looks into my eyes, searching for confirmation. I nod, and she turns away as tears fill her eyes.

I want to grab her, pull her to me and tell her it's going to be all right. I want to tell her that I love her, that I will always love her, but I can't. It wouldn't be right. I screwed up, not her. I don't deserve her.

"It's Liz. She's the potential host," she says softly, lifting her head, probably trying to blink back tears.

"Yes," is all I can manage to say. I have no tears. I don't deserve to even shed one. I'm revolting.

Abruptly, words pour out of her like water. "My best friend, Liz. She's the potential host, not me. She's the one meant to be with you and your family. It was her all along. It all makes so much more sense. Of course it's Liz. First, Liz telling me about a new boy at school, how there's something special about him when he enters a room, you two dancing at the prom as king and queen, and how you both look so perfect. It never even crossed my mind that it was Liz. Why would it?" Still turned away from me, she wipes at her cheeks with the back of her hand.

She whips back around. "Will, we had a good time, you and I. But now it's over. Obviously, we can't be together. I think you should go to Liz. Potential hosts are rare, right? Besides, Liz is a good person and would make a fine host. You two could be happy. You won't have to give up anything, and I know she finds you attractive."

What is she saying? I'm speechless. How can she be so calm? I certainly didn't expect this response. I thought she would lay into me...hit me...yell at me...something...something besides this! I don't want Liz! I want her!

She glances down for a second. "You'll have to work out her boyfriend issue, but I think it's obvious now that you were destined to find her, not me."

She tries to walk away, but I can't let go of her hand. "Wait, you don't understand—"

"I don't want to talk about this anymore, and I'm ready to go home. Just please do me a favor. Make her happy, and protect her. She means a lot to me," she says with finality.

She pulls her hand away and walks back into the house.

My voice catches in my throat as the first tear finally hits my cheek. My chondria recede into my chest as if to strengthen my heart as it breaks in two. They won't give up on her. But still, she's leaving, the love of my life, and she wants nothing to do with me or my chondria.

26

AS ONE DOOR CLOSES...

Marley

Will isn't at school on Monday, but Liz is there. As soon as I see her, it's too much to handle. I run the other way, tears stinging my eyes. Later, when she asks me what's wrong, I give the lamest excuse. Will and I had a fight, so we broke up. I also tell her it was my fault, not his. I don't want her to have a bad impression of him when they start dating, and I also don't want her to turn him down because of me. After trying to change the subject a few times, I realize she's on to me.

"Okay, enough. What's going on with you, Marley? I don't like this one bit. One minute you act like you're all in love with this guy, calling me late Saturday night asking if I will cover for you while you spend the night at his house, and now you two aren't speaking? You have to admit, that's a little messed up." She doesn't beat around the bush, ever. Then her eyes get really big with concern. "Oh my God, did he...hurt you?"

The shock of what she's implying rips through my body. He's the most honorable guy I've ever met. Knowing Will for such a short amount of time has changed my life forever. I mean...he just wouldn't! "Of course not! He would never do anything like that! Can we not talk about it anymore, please?" It's my last effort to stop the conversation.

She can tell I'm spent. The dark, puffy circles under my eyes give me away. It's very hard to keep up the pretense that everything is okay when I'm wearing those 'not sleeping' and crying badges.

"Okay, for now, but if you need me, you know that I'm always here for you no matter what, right?"

Even though I'm dying to tell her everything, I can't. I thank her for letting it go, and she hugs me. I hold my breath, blinking profusely. What is it about tears? Once you let them spill down your cheeks, they won't stop.

The rest of my day is simply going through the motions, pretending to listen in all my classes. There is one exception. English with Justin. I was nervous to talk to him because of how he feels about me. I did leave him kind of abruptly on the dance floor at prom. But so much has happened since then. He says something that completely takes me by surprise. He tells me that he misjudged Will, and he hopes I'm happy with him. Someone's had a complete turnaround, haven't they? I roll my eyes when he's not looking and slump deeper into my chair. I don't want to delve into my current love life, so I agree sheepishly. Then my mind drifts off, not wanting to talk at all.

During the last period of the day, Civics with Mrs. O'Leary, I've reached my limit. It's almost too much to think about, being sent to the office for Will, and meeting him for the first time in the nurse's office. After the final bell rings, I wave goodbye to Liz and sink down in my chair. I can't move. I'm overwhelmed with sadness. My mom always says time heals all wounds. It's what she used to say about my dad. Here's the thing—I don't know if this wound, this crushing pain, like my heart can barely thump to keep me alive, will ever heal. I look up through watery eyes that I can't keep under control, to find Mrs. O'Leary watching me from her desk, in the front of the room.

She looks thoughtful as she asks, "Marley, do you want to talk?"

I really want to talk to someone, anyone, but under the supernatural circumstances, I can't possibly do that. I'm stuck in my own misery. "No, Mrs. O'Leary," I say, hoping she drops it.

She gets up from her seat and walks toward my desk. "I think I might understand more than you realize." When she reaches the desk in front of me, she sits, bright blue fireflies swimming around in her eyes.

Oh...my...God! I wipe the tears off my cheeks with my sleeve, nervously. "Mrs. O'Leary, I had no idea that you...that you were..." I can't seem to string anything coherent together.

She takes my hand in hers. "My dear, there are quite a few of us out and about. It was not a coincidence that William Reed was assigned to this homeroom." She glances out the window as if remembering some fundamental thing. Then, her eyes rest back on mine. "I want to tell you a story. Do you have time?"

"Uh, sure," I say, eagerly reaching out for any sort of solace from the pain in my heart.

"*I was very much like you when I was identified as a potential host,*" she thinks, smiling.

I jump, startled by hearing her voice inside my head. I hadn't expected her to speak to me through thought, but her voice is so effortless and soothing. I smile back.

"*I didn't think I was special either. I was very shy and awkward around people. When I was very young, my parents found out that I had a weak heart, and I would eventually need a transplant at some point in my life. I was never allowed to go to the playground at recess or play kickball with the kids in the neighborhood. My parents were too afraid that my little heart would give out. Most of the kids didn't bother with me or made fun of me because of my weakness. After I got older, I found comfort in working at a local animal shelter. There were not only dogs and cats; there were birds, reptiles, and even a potbelly pig. The animals there didn't judge me, and they loved to sit with me while I took care of them. They became the only friends I wanted or needed.*" Mrs. O'Leary's face lights up as she speaks about the animals.

"*Then, one day, when I was an adult, a tracker approached me and told me that I was a potential host. I couldn't contain my excitement the first time I saw chondria swirling around in his eyes. I was already very fond of all creatures, but an extraterrestrial species? My goodness, I was captivated. After some candid conversations about the hosting world and their way of life, I decided that I would not make a good host. You see, I didn't believe I had any special abilities. I was terrible around other people, I was physically weak, and my best friend was a dog. I would be the most disappointing host that ever lived.*" She shakes her head, but a smile still lingers on her lips. "Does that sound familiar?"

It does. I know better than anyone how it feels to not have a purpose. I nod, thinking the tears might surface again, and blink a few times. "Yeah, it does. So why did you do it, I mean why did you become a host?"

Mrs. O'Leary puts her other hand on top of mine and thinks, "*Well, you see, I was very wrong. Sometimes what we see as weakness is, in fact, our biggest strength. Come with me to the window.*"

I stand and follow her over to the window, looking out at the trees in front of the parking lot. Okay, now what? Mrs. O'Leary closes her eyes for a moment, then opens them, focusing on something outside the window. She thinks, "*There, Marley. Look over at the maple tree to your left. What do you see?*" she asks, not taking her eyes away from it.

I see three chipmunks sitting in a row. How odd. They remind me of when I watched Will track. They scurry toward us and hop up on the windowsill. They sit in a row again, watching Mrs. O'Leary. She opens the window and reaches her hand out to one of the chipmunks, and he crawls into her palm. I can't believe what I'm seeing. She brings him inside and strokes his back. She looks at me with a huge grin and thinks, "*What do you think of my special ability?*"

"So wait, are you like an animal whisperer or something? How do you do that?" I ask excitedly. I wonder if I can pet the little guy too.

"*I can communicate with animals, Marley. I speak all of their languages. I am what our people call a creature host. I was the first host to realize this very remarkable ability. It's the best gift I could ever ask for. The day after I bonded with chondria, I went to the shelter and realized I could actually talk with my best friends. It was amazing. It gets even better too. I realized a few days later that my chondria repaired and strengthened my heart. I ran for the first time that day. I ran until my legs wouldn't take me any further. It was the best day of my life.*" She gazes down at the little chipmunk and asks, "Would you like to pet him? He likes a scratch on his back."

I reach out my hand slowly and, when he doesn't scurry away, I touch his little back. His fur is so soft and airy. His pelt feels amazing. After I pet him for a minute, Mrs. O'Leary places him back outside on the window sill and waves good-bye. All three chipmunks scurry off.

We continue to look out the window in silence until she says out loud, "I saw him the day he marked you. He loves you, you know? I believe he fell in love with you that very first day, and why wouldn't he? You're more special than you realize, Marley. Everything happens for a reason, and you should have faith in those who love and care for you. If you can do that, anything is possible. You need to follow you heart and believe."

All this time, and one of my favorite teachers at school is a host. She knew all along about Will and me. She's right too. He loves me, and I love him. We have to trust our feelings. "*Trust the voice inside...*"

"Thank you, Mrs. O'Leary. You have no idea how much you've helped me," I say, going back to my seat and grabbing my bag. I pause to hug her quickly before heading out of the room. It's going to take a little while to get there, and I have what I need in my bag.

I PULL into the Tumbling Run parking area a little after four in the afternoon. The dirt lot is vacant. I grab my bag and head toward the trail. I cross the bridge and begin my trek upward to get where I need to be. I start cautiously, nervous, but soon find myself clambering up the trail as fast as I can. I can't get to the waterfall fast enough.

Ten minutes later, I'm there, trying to catch my breath. Instinctively, I toss my bag to the ground and bend over, my hands on my thighs. In, out, in, out. Slowly, my breathing returns to normal. I glance up at the waterfall trickling down the rocks into the small pool on the ledge. This is it. This is where I fell in love with Will. I made my decision, and there's no turning back. I reach into my bag and pull out his onyx stone. Holding it in my hand, I roll it around and around until the little green streaks come to life. I close my eyes and think, "*Will, if only you could hear me...*"

Something quite amazing happens before I can finish the thought. I hear my name out loud.

I open my eyes and Will is there above me on the trail, his dark eyes aglow. I cover my heart with my hand; it's beating so fast at the sight of him. He's wearing the same dark circles under his eyes that I am. He hasn't been sleeping either.

"How did you get here? How did you know?" I ask.

He strides over to me and cups my face with his hands. "I wanted to feel close to you, so I came here. It's our special place. Marley, I love you, and I will only ever love you. You're my other half." He grabs my arms, pulling me in, and consumes me.

His mouth finds mine, and I'm spinning. Our mouths part and a fire lights inside of me. I wrap my arms around his neck and return every caress he offers with my own. He doesn't stop at my mouth either. His mouth trails down my jaw, then lower to my neck. It's like he can't get close enough. I gasp, never wanting to let go. His body feels so right. But the voice inside my head interrupts us, "*Tell him.*"

'*Stop it. Leave me alone,*' I tell the voice.

"*Tell him,*" the voice insists.

I pull away, breathing hard, trying to gather my thoughts.

"What's wrong?" he asks, and then as if remembering the severity of our situation, he adds, "Oh crap, I'm sorry, I shouldn't have kissed you. We can't be together like that. That was so stupid of me—"

"Wait, you're wrong. I only pulled away because I need to tell you something important. Today someone very special told me that I need to have faith in myself and follow my heart. Well, my heart will always lead me to you, and I need to trust in that. I believe that you and I are meant to be together. I don't have any intentions of only being your friend, or living without you, so—"

"Marley, don't move," Will says, his eyes intense on my shoulder.

"What? Why?" I ask, trying to look at my shoulder.

Will slides my shirt down, revealing my left shoulder. It's glowing again.

"Oh my God. How's this possible?" Will asks, in disbelief.

"I don't know. The glow faded a day after you marked me." I don't know whether to be frightened or elated.

"I've never seen anything like this before. It always fades." He traces his finger around the mark on my shoulder as it tingles under his touch.

"So what does it mean? Is there something wrong with me because I'm not a potential host or is this like a good thing?"

He smiles, reaching for me again. "I don't know, but it sure seems like a good sign. It's actually pretty amazing, but then so are you."

Then he's kissing me again, and I think I might combust from the heat our bodies are generating. It's going to happen. I grasp the front of his jacket and push it back off his shoulders. His mouth finds my neck as I reach for the bottom of his t-shirt. As soon as my fingers touch skin just above his jeans, he stops and pushes me away.

"What?"

"We can't."

"Oh, okay, I get it. You're not ready. Well, you know how I feel about needles, but I guess that way would be okay too."

"Marley, what are you talking about?"

Why is he confused? "You bonding me with chondria. What else would I be talking about?"

Will's eyebrows shoot up in alarm, and he shakes his head. "I will do no such thing! You could die!" Then he turns away, perhaps trying to come to grips with what I said.

As I reach to touch him, he quickly turns back around with glassy eyes, his chondria seeming to swim. "Look, you didn't give me a chance to tell you my plan at my house. I tried, but you were so upset. I thought you didn't want to be with me because you told me to go be with Liz. Plus, I did cause some pretty awful stuff to happen to you. But here's the thing, my chondria won't allow me to give up on you. Now your shoulder is glowing again. I don't know what it all means, but it's something. It's definitely something. What I'm trying to say is that I believe it too. It's you. There's something I've not been able to figure out about us...it's almost like I've met you..."

"...before," I finish his sentence. "I know. I feel it too."

"But, I refuse to bond you. I mean, what if it doesn't work? It's way too risky. Or are you saying you don't care if you die?"

Well, that's a little uncalled for. "Of course not! I'm not suicidal or anything. Jeez." I run my hand through my hair in frustration. This is going to be difficult to explain. How do I tell someone who has incredible abilities that I have a voice inside my head that's telling me I'm supposed to be a host? He'll think I'm crazy for sure. No, I can't go that route. "*Why not?*" the voice asks. *Because I just can't, that's why.*

I place my hands on his chest, forcing him to give me his complete attention. "Listen, I know this sounds totally crazy, but I think I'm supposed to be a host, and you and I are meant to be together. What if I'm special? I've thought about this, Will. I didn't think I had any special skills, until today. Look at my shoulder. There's the proof. What if I can learn to adapt to being a host? What if *that* is my special talent? It might mean that I could help other hosts or something. Maybe I could track with you and help with the bonding process. I don't know...I'm still trying to figure it all out. But here's the thing, I've been struggling, trying to figure out my path in life, and I'm telling you *this* is it." I take a much-needed breath before I dive into the hardest part. "I want you to bond me without a needle. I'll be fine. It will work, I know it." I drop my hands, but my eyes never leave his. There, I said it; I put it all out there. Now, will he understand?

He studies me for a minute as if evaluating what I'm proposing, and frowns. Oh crap. Well, I tried, right?

"Marley, I've been thinking about bonding you that way since I first set eyes on you. But that was when I thought you were a potential host. Now, I don't think it's fair to ask you to give up so much. Don't you see? That's why I told you I wanted to be friends. I didn't want you to be with someone who might not be able to give you everything you deserve. It wouldn't be fair." He turns toward the waterfall, perhaps looking for solace in the calming trickle of water on stone.

So that's it? I don't have a say? I don't think so, not in my world. I grab his arm and turn him back around. "Hey, this isn't only up to you, you know? I want it with all my heart, and I know I have a good shot at it working. If I didn't believe that, I wouldn't be here right now. So, if you mean what you say and you want to be with me as much as I want to be with you, then..." I can't think of what to say, I'm grasping for the words, so I blurt out the only thing that pops into my head, "...then grow a pair and let's agree to make it work." I mean every word, well, almost every word, and I have no intention of changing my mind.

A smile tugs at the corner of his mouth. "You're crazy, you know that? You always say the stuff that's in your head. No filter." He puts his hands on his hips and shakes his head, looking thoughtful.

I raise my eyebrows curiously, wishing I could read his mind.

He sighs. "But, I guess it's part of what I love about you. 'Grow a pair' huh?"

I laugh. "Well, it seemed like the right thing to say at the time."

He grabs my hand and draws me to him. "*I still think it's too risky. I won't agree to bond you right now. But, if you'll give me some time, I'll explore every possibility that might allow us to be together, if that's what you really want.*" He gently lifts my chin with his hand, leaning toward me so that our noses are almost touching. "Deal?"

He's always got to be in charge. God, it makes me want to scream and laugh at the same time. Still, it's better than nothing. Even if it means that I have him in my life for only a short time, it will be worth every minute. I smile playfully, looking into his firefly eyes. "Deal...for now."

EPILOGUE

A BIRTHDAY GIFT

Will

My parents and I have been planning a big celebration for Marley's birthday. We definitely have the backyard for it, and I've been working on it for weeks. Her good friends will all be here, including Liz, Becca, and the guy who doesn't like me much, Justin. I even invited A.J. for my sister, Anna. I can't understand what she sees in him. My dad is trying his hand at some Indian cuisine, Marley's favorite. Mr. Graham, the home-ec teacher, and his partner, Mr. Hernandez, are helping too. I also invited Mrs. O'Leary, knowing that Marley will be surprised to see some of our teachers here to celebrate with her. Some of my host friends who met Marley briefly will be here as well, including Aiden McConnell and Parker West.

It's a warm day, and I want everything to be perfect. My mom approaches me. "When should we expect the guest of honor?"

"Soon enough, Mom. I assume that everything is set for her gift?" I ask, hoping for no snags.

"Yes, I was given permission an hour ago. You're all set. What a thoughtful boy I have." She puts a hand into my floppy mess of hair, kissing me on the cheek.

"Okay, Mom," I say, rolling my eyes. Still, I love that she's supporting my relationship with Marley. It should be any minute now that she'll be here for a 'family dinner.' It's a lie, of course, to get her here. As soon as I don't think I can wait any longer, I hear her old Honda Civic pull up my driveway. The muffler is so loud it makes me laugh. Why does she love that car so much?

I shout, "Everyone! Quiet! She's coming!"

I walk through the house to the front door and open it. She's standing on the front porch wearing a long, purple tie-dye sundress with her hair down blowing around her perfect face. She looks amazing.

"Hi, babe. You look great. Come in," I say with as much coolness as I can muster.

"Hey, yourself. Why are you all dressed up?"

I look down at my suit. I guess I do look overdressed for a 'family dinner.' Oh well. "I wanted to look my best..." I grab her hand and lead her out back.

Everyone yells, "Happy Birthday!"

Marley smiles and buries her head in my shoulder. I love when she gets embarrassed like this. It's so adorable. She comes out from hiding and says, "Thanks, everyone, this is amazing!" and then she whispers so only I can hear, "you just wait until I get you alone later."

I kiss her cheek, wanting to do more, but there are a ton of people watching us.

Marley seems to enjoy everything I planned. After everyone leaves, I take her hand and lead her to the patio sofa. My parents and Anna all gather around. They are as excited as I am about my gift.

"Marley, I haven't given you a birthday present yet. What I want to give you is something I hope you will enjoy. So, here goes..." I glance around at my parents and Anna. I'm nervous.

My chondria swirl around my irises, sensing my anticipation. "I got permission to take you to the Annual Host Gathering this year. Would you do me the honor of attending with me?" I ask, holding my breath.

Nothing can prepare me for her response. Marley's eyes fill with tears, and she puts her head in her hands. Oh no, is this a terrible reminder about our situation? What have I done?

"Oh, I'm sorry. I didn't know..." I'm at a loss. I don't know what to say.

She looks up. Tears are spilling down her cheeks, but she's smiling. "Don't. I'm happy! It's the best present I've ever gotten."

She leans over and hugs me. I pull back and look into her eyes. I press my lips to hers, wondering how I got so lucky.

But then again, maybe luck didn't have anything to do with it...

READ ON FOR A SNEAK PEEK...

RAZERS Book 2 in the Fireflies *Trilogy By MELISSA KOBERLEIN*

Marley

Summertime in the Appalachians is so humid you can almost see heat rising off the pavement into the air, like a spectral mist. Ghosts don't exist, but aliens do, and they're living inside my boyfriend. I stretch my arms and yawn, my bare legs sticking to the leather seat of Will's sleek, black sports car, waiting for him to return from the large medical center stretched out before me. I'm not fond of hospitals, so I chose to stay in the car and watch the heat.

I jump as my phone rings and vibrates from inside the front pocket of my camo shorts. I reach for it and look down at the familiar name. "Hey, Mom, what's up?"

"Marley, where are you? I thought you were going to stay home today and help me paint the downstairs. When I got back from the store, you were gone."

I cringe and sink down into the seat. "I totally forgot. I'm out with Will on our way to go hiking. Can we please paint tomorrow?"

There's a pause that seems to last forever considering my mom is never at a loss for words.

"You know, Marley, you seem to forget a lot of things since you've been dating Will. Don't get me wrong, I like him, but that doesn't mean your responsibilities just go right out the window."

I can't deny that I've been a little forgetful since Will and I started dating last spring at the end of my junior year of high school. "Okay, Mom, I promise I'll be more responsible in the future. I really did forget."

"Well, last time I checked, you were very responsible. I also remember you complaining about a certain best friend not remembering things, and now it's *you* who has a selective memory."

This is also true. My best friend, Liz, is usually the forgetful one. I open my mouth to respond, but Mom's on a roll. "Look, I try not to ask you for much, and I want you to have your own life, but the summer only lasts so long. I won't see you for a while after next week because of your trip with Will and his family."

Will and his family, who are all alien hosts, invited me to go to Arizona with them for some kind of alien convention called the Annual Host Gathering, where they show off their alien abilities and compete in games. I'm the first non-host ever to be invited. Needless to say, I can't wait to go. Still, my mom's right, I won't be around for the remainder of the summer. I lean back against the seat, feeling dejected. I really wanted to go hiking. "I know, Mom. I'm sorry; I'll come home now."

The phone goes silent again. She's thinking about it. I twirl one of the curls at the nape of my neck in anticipation of her response.

"No..." She huffs, conceding. "It's fine. Can you be home by three?"

I lean forward, excitedly. "Yes, I promise, and I'll be ready to paint!" I hold my breath, hoping to be let off the hook.

"I guess that will work. But you have got to start being more responsible, Marley. If I didn't know better, I'd say that boy has some special power over you. See you at three, and not a minute later."

"Okay, thanks. Love you."

"Love you too. Stay hydrated, it's a hot one."

"I will, bye."

I smile and exhale. If my mom only knew...

About fifty years ago, Will's mom discovered a meteorite that contained aliens while hiking in the Appalachians. The aliens give humans special abilities and a longer lifespan. The only problem is that there aren't many humans who are compatible with chondria. Humans who are compatible are called potential hosts and can choose to be like Will. Ordinary humans aren't compatible and chondria kill them. Unfortunately, Will has placed me in the ordinary group.

I pull down the car visor, opening the mirror to check my face and hair. I can't help but smile and laugh. While I tend to wear little in the way of makeup and don't really feel the need for any, I do use a ton of product in my hair. I have no idea why I try, since my blonde hair is now a big cotton ball, poofy mess. Stupid humidity. I know Will loves when I wear it down, but I just can't today. I pull the black hair band from my wrist and comb my curls back with my fingers into a high ponytail. It's too hot anyway.

I flip the visor back into place and peer up at the medical center, wondering how much longer it will be. Dr. Arcanas, a host himself, requests blood donations from hosts in the area, and since Will hasn't donated for a while, we had to make a 'quick' stop. Every time I've seen blood in my life I've ended up flat on my back, and I don't see that changing anytime soon. Even thinking about Will with a needle in his arm right now makes me kinda dizzy. It's also a family joke since my mom's a nurse at Pine Grove General, the other medical center in Pine Grove. We're a small town, so we don't actually have a legitimate hospital.

I shift uncomfortably in my seat, bored, hoping it doesn't take too much longer. We are parked at the back of the building where there is only a small entrance. The door opens, but it's not Will. Instead, a group of patients wearing blue scrubs, gowns, and robes is being led out into the grass. I can tell by their sluggish movements that they're sedated or something. When the door finally closes, I count at least forty patients milling about on the lawn in front of the building.

Some of the patients sit on benches, rocking back and forth while others just keep walking around.

Then I see the one person I had hoped never to set eyes on again. My heart skips a beat and my jaw drops. These people aren't from the psych ward—they are Dr. Arcanas's patients.

Directly in front of Will's car, about ten feet away, is none other than Sam Wyatt. I recognize his light brown hair, intimidating height and build, and purple listless glowing eyes as he stares in my direction. The hair on the back of my neck stands up.

Sam and I have a history of sorts, none of it good. He's what Will's kind call a razer, a potential host bonded with chondria against his or her will, which means he's in a perpetual vegetative state only able to follow the directions of the host who bonded him.

I'm not sure if it's fortunate or unfortunate, but I killed that host. Of course, I didn't have a choice in the matter—Malcolm Durst was about to end my life or turn me into a razer like Sam. So I did what I had to do to survive. It was hard to think about afterward—killing someone, I mean—but I realized that sometimes life doesn't give you choices. Afterward, Will's sister, Anna, whose special ability is telekinesis, transferred all of Malcolm's chondria to Sam so they wouldn't die too. What that means, I haven't a clue. If Malcolm's chondria remember what I did, that wouldn't be good news for me. Based on the way he's looking at me right now, he knows exactly who I am.

All I want to do is slide into the driver's seat and get the hell out of here, but I can't seem to make my legs move. Instead, they're firmly stuck to the seat, getting slick on the leather as I begin to sweat, adrenaline flooding my limbs. Sam tilts his head, his eyes still fixed on mine. He lifts his face toward the sky, sniffing the air as if trying to detect a scent, like a wolf searching for prey. I've seen him do this before when he abducted me from the junior prom just a month ago. The same strangling, heart-wrenching fear I felt then seeps back into my chest now.

A few more patients stop dead in their tracks; their mouths drop open, and their hands twitch—no, convulse. The tremors seem to spread up their arms and into their chest and shoulders, finally shaking their heads. Slowly, one by one, their heads turn toward me. As soon as I see their eyes, I know—these aren't ordinary patients, they're razers. It's like a domino effect spreading outward. One by one, each patient turns their head in my direction. At the center is Sam. I cover my mouth, shocked by their behavior. Finally, every single razer on the lawn is motionless and staring at me. Two orderlies wearing white uniforms are telling jokes and smoking cigarettes by the door, completely unaware of what the patients are doing.

The razers slowly begin moving again, but now they are all moving in the same direction—toward me. Intuitively, I lock the doors. What the hell is going on? What's happening to them? What do they want? Is it Sam making them do this? I can't breathe. *Okay, slow down.* I've got to get a grip. I close my eyes.

Deep breaths. It's just your imagination. You had a bad experience. Sam is not after you. They are not after you. You're fine and safe inside Will's car. It's all in your head. You're fine. Will is going to be here in a minute. We'll go hiking, and it'll be a beautiful day. There's nothing to worry about. In and out, slow, *breathe.*

Without warning, the sound of glass breaking next to my head blasts me back to the present. Shards of glass fall on my lap. I scream and look at the passenger side window. The glass is gone, leaving a few slivers sticking up around the frame. Razers are everywhere. They have surrounded the car. Some are even climbing on the hood, making strangled, moaning sounds.

"Help!" I yell.

A middle-aged male razer with bluish glowing eyes and a dark buzz cut, receding on the top, reaches in and cuts his wrist on the broken glass. His wrist spurts warm, metallic-smelling red on my face, hair, and shirt. I scream some more while he groans and grabs my arm. Oh my God, he's trying to pull me out of the car! I slap at him a few times, but he won't let go. Damn, he's clamped on me tight for someone who is supposed to be in a vegetative state!

I reach for the onyx stone hanging around my neck, not only a gift from Will, but a pager of sorts if I ever need him. "No! Stop it! Let me go! Help! Someone! Please help me!"

The next thing I hear is Will's voice in my head; a gift afforded to all alien hosts. *"Marley! I'm coming, hang on!"*

The orderlies finally show up and begin pulling razers off the hood of the car. The one who has a death grip on my arm stops pulling but doesn't let go. He leans in and stares at me, his face right next to mine. I cringe, bracing for whatever is to come next. But instead of violence, his pupils focus, the eerie blue glow subsiding to reveal one tiny blue chondria swimming in a circle around his left iris. I can't look away. I'm transfixed. It's as if that one blue chondria is trying to tell me something. *What? What is it? What do you want?*

There's a banging coming from the driver's side. Slowly,

surreally, I turn my head toward Will. I reach the electronic unlock button on my side, and the driver's side door opens.

Through a haze, I hear Will's voice. "Marley! Jesus, you're covered in blood!"

I turn back toward the razer and catch a glimpse of Agent Rushmore behind him, pulling him away. I hear a strange voice in my head, "*Need you,*" and the razer is gone.

ABOUT THE AUTHOR

Melissa Koberlein is a professor of communication and publishing in eastern Pennsylvania where she lives with her husband and their two daughters. She enjoys reading and writing about the spectacular, sci-fi, technology, and romance. Her passion for stories comes from an imaginative childhood where every day ended with a book. *Ashwater* is her newest young adult series. You can read the rest of her first series, *Fireflies*, available from Amazon and other retail outlets.

facebook.com/mekoberlein

twitter.com/melkoberlein

instagram.com/melkoberlein

ALSO BY MELISSA KOBERLEIN

"Raven's Sphere will make you happy, sad and laugh the entire book. This is a must read and a true page turner."

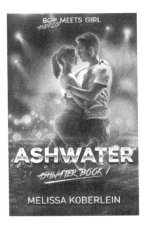

"Ashwater by Melissa Koberlein is a must-read. If your looking for a good read filled with sci-fi, humor, romance and twists then this book is what you need."

Made in the USA
Middletown, DE
14 April 2022

64224394R00154